**Mitch wondered what it was
about the woman
that fascinated him.**

She wasn't even vaguely the kind of woman who usually caught his eye. He liked his women the same way he liked his money: easy and uncomplicated. Leigh Bramwell didn't look easy, and she sure as hell wasn't making his life uncomplicated.

He also liked his women sleek, and the peek he'd gotten of the body beneath her down-filled parka suggested it could more aptly be described as soft and gently rounded. Suddenly even that appealed to him as it never had before.

Hell, he thought, shifting restlessly, he'd been without a woman for too long. That must explain the insane way he was acting...

With two young sons at home, former teacher **Liz Grady** *decided she needed to do more than cook, clean, and fingerpaint. An avid romance reader, she tried her hand at writing. She credits much of her success in her new career to her very supportive husband and her adaptable children. When a relative once commented, "Most people learn to distinguish fantasy from reality by age five; Liz never has," Liz's response was, "I hope I never do!" She and her family live in Rhode Island.*

Dear Reader:

The August books are here—and what a terrific bunch they are!

In *Such Rough Splendor* (#280), Cinda Richards—who delighted us with her zany *This Side of Paradise* (#237)—has penned a romance that we think will become a classic of the genre. The best elements of romance come together with superlative skill in this warm, funny, poignant tale of love and healing, as divorcée Amelia Taylor makes war and peace with, in her words, "the biggest, dumbest cow puncher she's ever clapped eyes on." Houston "Mac" McDade will live on in your memories as one of the most original and irresistible heroes you've ever had the good fortune to lock horns with!

Sarah Crewe explores the complexities of pursuit and revenge in *Windflame* (#281), a strong follow-up to her earlier romances. Melissa Markham's job as college fundraiser forces her to pursue wealthy Dakin Quarry for his money, but her immediate attraction to him vastly complicates the situation. Distrust, scandal, revenge, and Dakin's own fatal passion for Melissa combine to form a compelling, tension-filled love story set against a quiet college campus.

Lauren Fox's zest-filled, lusty romance *Storm and Starlight* (#282) will catch you up and whirl you away—just as Eric Nielson does to Maggie McGuire when she arrives to investigate the proposed expansion of his satellite-dish manufacturing company. There's never a dull moment as Maggie struggles to curb Eric's exuberant excesses and Eric gets Maggie into one outrageous situation after another. The banter flies fast and furious and the action's nonstop as these two forceful characters love and live with passionate energy.

In *Heart of the Hunter* (#283), Liz Grady has outdone herself, creating Mitch Cutter, a hard-boiled, gun-slinging bounty hunter who fears nothing except love, and Leigh Bramwell, a dyed-in-the-wool romantic with a long streak of cowardice. Never has a man so inept with "nice girls"—a man whose only way of loving a woman is by deceiving and possessing her—seemed so heart-wrenchingly appealing. *Heart of the Hunter* is a romance you'll read with excitement—and cherish for years to come.

Lucky's Woman (#284) will tug at your heartstrings and make you smile through your tears as only a romance by Delaney Devers can. With roughhewn "Lucky" Verret and ladylike Summer Jordan, Delaney creates a love so potent it has the power to destroy the very hearts it fills. You'll shiver with Summer as she braves mosquitoes, mud-creatures, and mayhem in the Louisiana swamp she loathes, in order to prove her loyalty to stubborn-as-sin Lucky. You'll ache with Lucky as he hides his longing from the woman he secretly cherishes but fears he cannot trust. All of you who raved about Delaney's *The Heart Victorious* (TO HAVE AND TO HOLD #40) and asked for more will find *Lucky's Woman* just the treat you've been waiting for.

Finally, SECOND CHANCE AT LOVE is pleased and proud to introduce a stunning new talent—Elizabeth N. Kary, author of *Portrait of a Lady* (#285). Here is an adult romance in the best sense of the word, the story of two complex characters whose struggles to trust and understand each other lead to an intimacy that's deep and powerfully satisfying. The maturity of Elizabeth's characters, the elegance of her writing style, and the page-turning quality of her story all set *Portrait of a Lady* apart as truly special. Don't miss the debut of this wonderful writer—and don't miss her first historical romance, *Love, Honor and Betray,* to be published by Berkley in January. This epic adventure and passionate love story set during the War of 1812 is destined to establish Elizabeth N. Kary as a romance writer of stature!

Enjoy these August romances and please keep your letters and questionnaires coming. We love reading them.

Best,

Ellen Edwards

Ellen Edwards, Senior Editor
SECOND CHANCE AT LOVE
The Berkley Publishing Group
200 Madison Avenue
New York, NY 10016

Second Chance at Love

HEART OF THE HUNTER

LIZ GRADY

**SECOND CHANCE AT LOVE
BOOK**

HEART OF THE HUNTER

Requests for permission to make copies of any part of the work should be mailed to: Permissions, Second Chance at Love, The Berkley Publishing Group, 200 Madison Avenue, New York, NY 10016.

First edition published August 1985

First printing

"Second Chance at Love" and the butterfly emblem are trademarks belonging to Jove Publications, Inc.

Printed in the United States of America

Second Chance at Love books are published by
The Berkley Publishing Group
200 Madison Avenue, New York, NY 10016

For my editor, Leslie Kazanjian,
whose subtle suggestions
invariably make me
write a better book

Chapter One

MITCH CUTTER HAD to force himself to step from the frosty February air into the shop bearing the elaborately scrolled emblem of DeMarco Jewelers—just as he'd had to force himself every step of the way there.

Pausing a few feet inside the front door, he tugged off his black leather gloves and ran a slightly amused, vastly critical gaze over the plush, cream-colored carpeting and the crystal chandeliers that spilled soft white light onto the riches nestled on beds of black velvet below. Scattered strategically behind the display cases was a small army of attentive salesmen, smilingly awaiting the bidding of the women who browsed amid the gold and jewels—women who wore more varieties of fur than Mitch had known existed.

Amazing, he thought with a fresh surge of disgust, what even the most tainted money could buy. An illusion of respectability, the patronage of society's finest, and maybe even him . . . if the price was right and the job not as dirty as most of DeMarco's dealings. Deciding the time had come to put a stop to this wondering about why DeMarco would ask to meet with him of all people, Mitch guided his long, aggressive stride toward the office tucked discreetly in the far corner of the showroom.

A burly young man sat at the desk in the outer office, looking more suited to the role of sergeant-at-arms than secretary. He glanced up when Mitch's lean, six-foot-two frame appeared in the doorway, straightening in a reflex response to the air of leashed power Mitch wore as casually as his clothes.

"I'm Mitch Cutter," he announced curtly. "I believe Mr. DeMarco is expecting me."

Obviously Mr. DeMarco was, for with a slight frown at the disrespectful emphasis Mitch put on the title *mister,* the young man stood and moved to the ornate mahogany door behind him.

"Mr. DeMarco," he said, edging it open after a perfunctory knock, "Cutter is here."

"Good!" responded an irritatingly jovial voice from Mitch's past. "Let him in."

Mitch was already across the narrow room, sweeping past the glaring lackey to plant his booted feet directly in front of Mr. Edward "Track Rat" DeMarco's massive desk.

"DeMarco," he said, inclining his dark head in meager acknowledgment. His gray eyes remained as hard and cold as gunmetal.

The older man nodded with a smile that really wasn't one. "Cutter."

Five years hadn't changed some things at all, Mitch thought. They were still adversaries at heart, instinctively on guard, eyeing each other like pit bulls in a ring. Other things had changed drastically. Like Mitch's profession, which no longer automatically put them on diametrically opposed sides of every issue. And DeMarco himself had changed from the fat, sleazy rat who used to hang around the racetrack lending money to suckers who had to repay it, win or lose, at a phenomenal interest rate. Now he was a fat, sleazy rat who sat in a posh office and let others do his lending—and his collecting.

"You've changed, DeMarco," Mitch remarked, his lips twisting into a sneer his dark beard and mustache in no way disguised. "And come a long way from the days of fleecing drunks and old ladies out at the track."

"I wish I could say the same for you." DeMarco's fleshy cheeks puffed up, and his gaze narrowed as it slid from Mitch's creased leather flight jacket to his faded black denims. "You were much better dressed as Rhode Island's most obnoxious detective than as a—what is it you bounty hunters like to call yourselves nowadays? Recovery agents?"

Mitch shrugged carelessly. "Call me whatever you please. I'm not in the PR business."

"No, you never were." His chuckle had a grating, insinuating quality. "You're a hunter—one of the best. That's why I called you. I want you to do some hunting for me, Cutter. A piece of cake of a job—shouldn't take you more than a couple of days and no complications. Interested in hearing the price I'm willing to pay?"

"I'm more interested in hearing about the prey you expect me to hunt."

"That's what I like: a man who loves his job."

"It's not *my* job yet, DeMarco. Unlike you, there are some things I won't do for money—like break the law."

The other man's thick gray brows levered up. "That's odd. I seem to remember some shakedowns and arm-twisting back in the old days that weren't quite legal, badge or no badge."

"Maybe I prefer to honor my own interpretation of the law," Mitch parried, one broad shoulder lifting in a negligent shrug.

"As do I," lunged DeMarco, eyes gleaming ferally. "I think maybe we're more alike than you'd like to believe, Cutter."

Mitch elected to ignore the repulsive suggestion.

"The prey, DeMarco," he prodded firmly. "Who is it you want tracked down so badly you're willing to pay *me* to do it when you have a dozen goons on your payroll who could handle a piece of cake of a job?"

"A woman, of course," he replied, lifting a photo from his desk and extending it to Mitch. "This woman. Her name is Leigh Bramwell and we're . . . involved." He chuckled obscenely. "We had a little spat a few days ago and she—Leigh—took off. You know how broads are."

Mitch didn't answer, but simply stared at the snapshot in his hand. The woman in the photo looked to be in her mid-twenties, average height, and was dressed in snug jeans and a bulky yellow sweater. She wasn't beautiful or glamorous, and judging by the free-falling waves of dark hair that tumbled over her shoulders, the untweezed eyebrows, and the barely made-up face captured before him, she didn't much try to be.

"Did you take this picture?" he asked DeMarco.

"What? Oh, yeah, sure. One day a few months ago."

"Where?" Mitch looked up from the picture in time to see DeMarco squirm satisfyingly in his overstuffed swivel chair.

"How the hell should I remember?" he snapped. "Some

apple orchard up in Scituate. I can't recall exactly where. Does it matter?"

"No," Mitch responded blandly, letting his gaze drop to the photo once more.

Anyone could tell it had been taken at an orchard from the rows of fruit-laden trees in the background and the basket full of apples beside the woman. A familiar wariness began to creep through him, starting deep in his belly. Somehow he couldn't picture DeMarco whiling away a crisp fall day picking apples. In fact, he couldn't picture him doing anything at all with the somewhat innocent-looking Leigh Bramwell.

He flipped the photo back onto the desk. "No deal, DeMarco. Hunting down wayward lovers and hauling them home doesn't appeal to me."

"Does five thousand dollars appeal to you?"

It did. And Mitch felt a ripple of self-disgust along with his renewed interest. While he had a distinct lack of interest in the material things money could buy, he had a deep, ingrained respect for security and independence. Five thousand dollars could buy a good-sized chunk of security for a man with minimal needs and a vocation whose next paycheck was as unpredictable as its hours.

"What if the lady is dead-set against coming back to you?" he asked, his voice suggesting that was not only possible but probable if the woman was even remotely sane. "I won't bind and gag her and drag her back to your bed even for fifty thousand. The prospect of playing John Alden to your Miles Standish is revolting enough."

"I don't even know those guys," DeMarco replied with an impatient sweep of his arm. "Besides, no one's asking you to drag anyone anywhere. I just want you to find her; then you give me a call, and I'll take it from there. You know, make it up with her."

"You just want to know where she is?" Mitch asked, his eyes narrowing with outright incredulity. "That's it?"

DeMarco nodded.

That shed a slightly less offensive light on Mitch's role in the whole thing—and increased the gut-level skepticism he'd walked in with.

"Then why not have one of your boys out front do the leg work and save yourself a bundle?"

The older man's jowels settled into a sneer. "Come on, Cutter, let's not play games. You saw that truck parked out front, the one that stands out like a sore thumb simply because it's so damned unremarkable. The Feds are about as subtle as a fox in a hen house, but they're diligent. They've got a tail on me and everyone who works for me, gearing up for a major grand jury offensive, rumor has it."

"In that case they might well tail me when I stroll out of here."

"Not when you leave carrying the specially gift-wrapped box that's waiting at the front counter for you. You'll simply look like a discriminating shopper," he explained, obviously proud of his ingenuity. "If I chanced sending one of my men after Leigh, she could end up being dragged into this whole mess, and I don't want that. Especially since it would probably mean my wife's hearing about our little . . . arrangement."

"Somehow I find it impossible to work up any real sympathy for you," Mitch responded grimly.

"I don't want your sympathy. I want your talent as a hunter. That's what you sell, isn't it? And that's what I'm offering to buy."

Mitch met his gaze levelly, the hard, chiseled planes

of his face set in a mask of cool professionalism, concealing the turmoil within. The creep had that right at least. He did make his living selling his highly developed skills as a hunter. He knew when he resigned from the state police force and started out on his own that he would be dealing with clients whose character and motives weren't always of the highest quality, and he'd long ago stopped asking questions—as long as his part in the deal didn't threaten to earn him a nice long vacation in the state prison.

If DeMarco really was involved with this Bramwell woman, and if they really had had a fight, how much harm could there be in letting him know where she was so he could take a stab at making amends? Maybe he would even tip her off at the same time so she could bolt again if she wanted to. After all, if he refused the job, DeMarco would just find someone else to do it, Mitch thought, deciding not to refuse and knowing he was rationalizing like hell.

Like the vulture he was, DeMarco seemed to sense his opponent's weakening resolve. "You can take the picture with you so you can be sure it's her when you find her. And here's a list of other things that might help: her local address, the names of some friends and a sister who lives in Maine somewhere. And twenty-five hundred up front." He folded his sausagelike fingers across his stomach and rocked confidently in his chair. "Any questions?"

Mitch palmed the snapshot and envelope DeMarco thrust across the desk and tucked them inside his jacket. "Yeah, one. Why are you willing to part with so much ill-gotten cash for such a slight service?"

"Simple. Love makes a man do foolish things."

"Really?" Mitch countered, meeting the man's leering

grin with an expression that was cold and emotionless and totally genuine. "I wouldn't know."

By the following afternoon, the snapshot was dog-eared from being pulled out of Mitch's pocket and scrutinized so often, far more often than was necessary from a professional standpoint. The more he stared at it, the more he wondered how someone who looked as wholesome as Leigh Bramwell could possibly be mixed up with someone like DeMarco. And the more he came to think of her as a woman first and his prey second.

It was an unfamiliar distinction for him to make when he was working and, Mitch realized, a potentially dangerous one—even if the assignment did seem to be panning out to be as simple as the man paying him had claimed. As was often the case, a combination of luck and timing delivered a crucial piece of information directly into his lap.

He'd spent the first day of his search trying to question any friends or co-workers he could turn up. A touchy proposition, since friends always had to be approached cautiously, and Leigh Bramwell didn't have any co-workers. She was, he learned from a chatty neighbor of hers, in the process of renovating her newly purchased home on the waterfront in Jamestown, with plans to open it as a bed-and-breakfast inn come spring.

On his second drive past the turreted stone dwelling he lucked out and encountered a local handyman leaning on the doorbell with as much luck as he'd had a few hours earlier. Mitch quickly joined him in front of the imposing arched doorway. No, the man had no idea where the crazy lady who wanted a railing with antique finials constructed on the second-floor balcony was, but she'd better be there in the morning, he declared, or his crew would just go ahead and do the job as they saw fit.

Acting on a hunch that, lover's spat or no, a woman pouring all this money and time into a new business would either be there to see that the job was done her way or send someone to ride herd for her, Mitch returned bright and early the following morning and parked a little way down the narrow street to wait. It payed off. A tall, sandy-haired man in his twenties arrived just after eight, letting himself in with a key.

After a carefully timed wait Mitch ambled up to the front door and discovered that Leigh Bramwell's obliging friend was gullible as well. He bought every word of Mitch's story about being a painting contractor who needed to know Miss Bramwell's decision on the trim colors right away, and in a matter of minutes Mitch had garnered the information that his quarry was staying at her sister's house for a few days while the sister and her husband were away on business.

The unsuspecting friend even supplied him with the telephone number there, a number Mitch had no intention of using. Phoning to verify that she was really staying at her sister's would be the easy thing to do. However, it wouldn't be the cautious thing to do, and a long time ago Mitch had learned the hard, painful way that in this business it paid to be cautious. Thirty minutes later, he had gassed up the Land Rover at a self-service station and was headed north on Route 95 toward Eliot, Maine.

The two-and-a-half-hour drive gave him plenty of time to think, and most of the thoughts that drifted through his mind didn't please him. He found himself volleying between a rather disgusted acceptance of the fact that Leigh Bramwell was really DeMarco's mistress, and the niggling feeling that the man had been lying through his teeth about the whole thing. Somewhere just over the

New Hampshire state line he decided to employ a well-honed talent for thought control and stop thinking about it, period. He'd already gone and accepted the job, and until he learned differently he would act on the assumption that the woman was exactly what he'd been told she was.

That only served to leave his mind free to tussle with a question that proved even more nettling. He wondered if money was the reason Leigh Bramwell was sleeping with a sleazy man old enough to be her father—money to finance the renovations on that stone hulk that looked like some Norman castle. How much did a castle cost these days? he mused. Probably a hell of a lot more than she'd been able to borrow from a reputable bank. Working interest payments off on your back certainly wasn't a novel approach in DeMarco's circles, but for reasons he chose not to explore, the notion suddenly irritated Mitch. Hell, this whole scene irritated him, and he'd be glad when he could collect the rest of his fee and be done with it.

Veering off the highway at the Eliot exit, he pulled into the parking lot of the first restaurant he came to, about a mile down the road. It wasn't really a restaurant, more of a small grocery store with a snack bar off to one side. It was the sort of place that saved the locals in this remote country area from driving into the more congested, touristy town of Portsmouth every time they needed a quart of milk. Mitch wasn't concerned with the lack of atmosphere. All he wanted was a sandwich, a cup of hot coffee, and directions to 13 Briarwood Drive.

He also wasn't consciously looking for the blue Honda Prelude with license plate LB 223 when he spotted it on the opposite side of the lot. He didn't have to. Like any good hunter, he absorbed all known details and habits of his quarry into his subconscious and lived with them, night and day, until the hunt was over. He didn't even break stride as he continued toward the entrance, or stare unduly at the car he knew belonged to Leigh Bramwell. He merely noted automatically that the roof and trunk were dusted with the light snow that had fallen this far north overnight.

But in every part of his body, a familiar reaction was taking place. Adrenaline began pumping furiously in preparation for whatever might happen. His stance, which still appeared loose limbed and negligent, concealed a musculature that was actually tensed and poised, ready to respond to any command his heightened senses might deliver. He no longer had any desire for coffee or a sandwich, and he thrust aside the knowledge that the smart thing, the *cautious* thing to do would be to wait in his car and follow her back to her sister's house before making the call to DeMarco that would conclude their deal. There was really no good, professional reason for him to enter the restaurant for his first flesh-and-blood glimpse of the woman he'd been tracking. But Mitch kept moving anyway, too caught up in the hunt to stop and figure out exactly what the unfamiliar emotion was that was propelling him inside.

The only patrons seated at the horseshoe-shaped, Formica-topped counter were an elderly man and a teenage couple who were thoroughly engrossed in each other. Mitch instinctively moved to take one of the stools facing the grocery section, where Leigh Bramwell had to be. He watched with studied nonchalance, ordering black coffee without glancing at the menu, and had just lifted the mug to his lips when she stepped from behind a rack of canned goods and headed straight for the cash register fifteen feet away from him.

Mitch felt the scalding hot coffee lodge in his throat along with his breath, and only sheer willpower kept him from spitting it back into the mug. Staring at her, he experienced an odd, rippling sensation, somewhere between déjà vu and fate—two notions he in no way believed in. He wasn't sure why he experienced it, and he didn't care, he told himself, grappling for the familiar feeling of professional detachment. All he cared about was that the woman chatting amiably with the clerk ringing up her groceries was the same woman whose photograph rested against his chest. The woman who was going to earn him a cool five thousand dollars.

His first impression of her had been right, he noted, taking another, more careful sip and letting it roll down his scorched throat. She was neither beautiful nor glamorous. Her black corduroy jeans and rose parka were nothing but a cold-weather version of what she wore in the photo. Her hair was the same, too, cascading several inches past her shoulders in loose waves that had more to do with nature than with curlers, he was certain. True, it radiated all sorts of rust and amber lights the camera had missed. And her eyes were blue. So blue that even at this distance in the restaurant's harsh light they made an image of summer skies flicker through his brain.

The camera had failed on other scores as well, overlooking factors that his razor-sharp eye for detail did not. Things like the intelligence reflected in her wide-set eyes and the spirited angle of her jaw and the humor revealed by perfectly shaped lips that curved easily and often into a smile. Reluctantly, Mitch dropped his gaze from her face to the items she had just paid for, which the clerk was now efficiently piling into two brown paper bags. He scanned them absorbedly, automatically registering that most of the odd assortment of cans, boxes, and jars were not what he would consider staples for a woman hiding out by herself for a few days.

As the last jar of artichoke hearts disappeared into the bag, he lifted his gaze to find Leigh Bramwell watching him watch her. At that moment her clear blue eyes reflected something besides intelligence, something that started as caution and quickly escalated to a glimmer of raw panic. The friendly smile that had been there for the past few minutes dissolved into a tight line in a face that was suddenly drained of color. Wrenching both bags from the counter with an agile strength he figured was probably equal parts adrenaline and desperation, she practically ran for the door.

Mitch stayed put, signaling the waitress for a refill. There was no way he could follow her home now. The lady had obviously been primed for the possibility of someone's coming to look for her and had correctly interpreted his staring as something other than the interest of a casual observer. Hightailing it out of there after her would probably send her driving around in panicked circles. He would have to revert to his original plan and secure directions to her sister's house on his own. A quick drive by to check if her car was there should be enough to satisfy his professional compulsion to be certain. Then he could make the call and probably be home in time for dinner. If Leigh Bramwell turned out to be as smart as she looked, taking his appearance as a warning and disappearing before DeMarco arrived to collect her, that was lover boy's problem.

The prospect made Mitch's lips twist into a hard smile as he dropped some coins onto the counter and walked out.

Briarwood Drive was only a short distance from the restaurant, and soon the Land Rover coasted to a halt at the top of a small rise that afforded its driver a clear view of the green raised-ranch style home bearing the brass number 13 on the mailbox. He'd already driven by twice, slowly, and determined that the Prelude was parked in the double garage beneath the house. The hunt was finished, and there was nothing to stop him from calling DeMarco and telling him where he could find his errant lover.

Nothing, that is, except the persistent churning in his gut that kept insisting—over his determined attempts to convince himself it was none of his business—that Leigh Bramwell was not DeMarco's lover. Maybe, he speculated as he slouched in the seat, eyes trained unwaveringly on the house and the rustic yard surrounding it, maybe DeMarco wanted her for a lover and that's why she'd fled. With a frown he discarded the theory. The unsophisticated Ms. Bramwell was not the kind of woman to inspire a man to squander five thousand dollars just on a whim.

Even as he dismissed her as being less than siren material on a physical level, Mitch wondered what it was about the woman that fascinated him. Because much as he'd been trying to deny it, he was fascinated. Even more so since his glimpse of her back at the restaurant. She wasn't even vaguely the kind of woman who usually caught his eye. He liked his women the same way he liked his money: easy and uncomplicated. Leigh Bramwell didn't look easy, and she sure as hell wasn't making his life uncomplicated. He also liked his women sleek, and the peek he'd gotten of the body beneath her down-filled parka suggested it could more aptly be described as soft and gently rounded. Suddenly even that appealed to him as it never had before.

Hell, he thought, shifting restlessly in the seat, he'd

been without a woman for too long. That must explain the insane way he was acting. That and a natural abhorrence of doing a favor for DeMarco, regardless of the price tag. Straightening with renewed determination, he reached to start the Jeep just as the soft, fascinating body in the rose-colored parka emerged through the side door. The engine remained silent.

Leigh Bramwell hurried along the path to the six-foot stack of firewood by the side of the shed. Methodically stamping her feet against the cold the whole while, she loaded as much wood as she could into the canvas sling she was carrying. Firewood. That meant she was staying, in spite of the scare she'd gotten from seeing him. Was the woman gutsy, Mitch brooded, or stupid? Or did she simply want to be found?

As he watched, she thrust the loaded sling inside the doorway, then turned and stepped off the path to where last night's storm had dumped a thick layer of fresh snow. He immediately squinted his eyes, as much in disbelief as against the glare of the late afternoon sun. Even as he was thinking she couldn't be, she did—unceremoniously plopping her backside down in the snow, then stretching out flat on her back. In a graceful motion that stirred some long-forgotten memories in Mitch, she fluttered her arms up and down before scooting back up and turning to survey the image she'd created.

In the moment that followed, Mitch felt all his carefully cultivated professional instincts overridden by a rush of feeling that was elemental and very, very alien. Money be damned—there was just no way he could coldly hand over to DeMarco a woman who made angels in the snow.

Chapter Two

As HE RANG the doorbell, Mitch had no clear idea of what he was going to say, but he needed to know more about the woman inside before he could decide what to do next. The second she pulled open the heavy inner door, he did the same to the glass-paned storm door and in a quick, well-practiced move planted one boot directly over the threshold to prevent her from slamming the door shut on him. That didn't stop her from trying.

Leigh Bramwell shoved the door toward him, and the frightened expression he'd seen back in the restaurant reappeared on her face. But as her eyes fell to the foot so effortlessly foiling her attempts, something else flickered in the depths of her startling blue eyes. Anger.

"What do you want?" she demanded, a revealing catch in her soft voice.

Mitch attempted a polite, reassuring smile, but such civilities didn't come easy to him. "My name is Mitch

Cutter, Ms. Bramwell, and I'd like to talk to you for a minute."

"Why?"

"Because a man named Eddie DeMarco is looking for you and—"

That was as far as he got in his attempt to find out if honesty was always the best policy. In this case it obviously wasn't. A craftily worded subterfuge probably would have spared both of them the scene that followed.

The apricot tint of Leigh Bramwell's cheeks disappeared, leaving her face nearly as white and pathetic looking as the knuckles of her hand clenching the edge of the door for support.

"No . . . please," she began haltingly in a tone that made Mitch feel like Jack the Ripper reincarnated. "I don't have the money yet, but I can get it. You have to believe me. I promise I'll pay back my part of it as soon as I can, with whatever interest Mr. DeMarco wants. You have to—"

Instinctively Mitch raised his hand, not knowing quite how to stem her pleading.

"No, don't touch me," she gasped, drawing back a step, eyes wide and horrified now. "It's not going to help anything if you work me over—I can't earn the money in a hospital bed . . . or"—she swallowed hard—"the morgue. Besides, I'll scream, and the neighbors will all come running—this is a very close-knit community. And your car is parked right out front there in full view. And I also left a document explaining where I am and the whole story hidden back in Rhode Island to be read if anything happens to me. It implicates your boss DeMarco fully."

The words *DeMarco isn't my boss* died on Mitch's lips, leaving a bitter aftertaste. Work her over? The morgue? Hidden documents? Lord, the woman was a walking victim of too many cheap detective shows. He felt a sudden wave of amusement, but she was obviously taking the whole thing very seriously.

She was also obviously not merely a piqued mistress playing an elaborate game of hide-and-seek, and Mitch wondered where that left him. Unemployed, he decided. He should just get back into the Jeep, return DeMarco's cash advance, and put this whole mess behind him. But as he stared into Leigh Bramwell's wide, vulnerable eyes and listened to her halting, breathless attempts to talk herself out of being "worked over," he had an odd feeling he wasn't going to end up doing anything like that.

He knew now that whatever reason DeMarco had for wanting her found had to do with business, not pleasure. And the stakes must be high if he was willing to pay five thousand dollars to get his hands on her. That reason might well have to do with the federal investigation that was going on, but if she knew anything about that, she was not in any shape to discuss it rationally. Especially, he realized ruefully, once she discovered he really was working for DeMarco. *Had been* working for him, he qualified, and immediately felt better than he had in days.

Abruptly, he became aware of a sound other than her disjointed explanation of how she planned to pay back the money she owed in installments, beginning as soon as her inn opened in the spring. He angled his head and discovered that the scraping noise was being made by a man who'd appeared across the street to calmly shovel his already impeccable driveway, training one eye on the drama being played out over here. It occurred to Mitch that he'd waited long enough for Leigh Bramwell to invite him inside.

Stepping forward, he hitched his arm around her

shoulders in a gesture intended to look romantically inspired and pressed her back into the hallway, kicking the door closed behind them in the process. She stared up at him, speechless, her vocal cords apparently stalled somewhere between rambling and screaming, and he took advantage of her silence to get in a little explaining of his own.

"Ms. Bramwell, please calm down. There's no reason for you to be afraid of me." She trembled against him, reminding him that his arm was still around her. He hesitated a second before dropping it. "You obviously think I work for DeMarco and that I'm here to collect the money you owe him. I'm not."

Fear and desperation and wariness still swirled in her eyes, but there was a hint of relief there now as well.

"You're not?" she breathed tentatively.

Mitch shook his head.

Her straight white teeth released their grip on her bottom lip, leaving small light marks on the smooth red surface. Mitch watched them fade slowly. Then he shifted his gaze up to find her peering at him with a hopeful appeal that tore at a responsive chord inside, one he hadn't been bothered by in a long time.

"Then why *are* you here?" she asked. "What do you want with me?"

I don't know. The answer rose automatically in his mind, confusing and unbidden, and Mitch pushed it aside. He made another stab at a smile, hoping to wipe a little more of the distrust from her eyes while he searched for some way to eradicate it completely. What, he wondered, would it take to convince this woman that he wanted to protect her, not hurt her? Without bothering to wonder why that was suddenly so damned important to him, he slowly reached into his back pocket for the counterfeit I.D. that was just one of the tricks of his trade.

"I work for the federal government," he informed her smoothly, holding the black leather case open and aloft. "And if you have a problem with Eddie DeMarco, believe me, I'm on your side."

Leigh felt a shiver of relief course through her, and it suddenly became much easier to breathe. The I.D. he seemed willing to let her examine at length looked authentic enough—exactly like those the two agents who visited her at home a few days ago had produced. Of course, she admitted with a stab of frustration, she probably wouldn't know the difference anyway. She'd discovered during the past week that she possessed a disgusting naïveté about human nature in general and the dangerous world she'd suddenly been thrust into in particular.

That's why she wasn't sure whether to believe Mitchell R. Cutter's claim or not. He certainly didn't look like the middle-aged, conservatively dressed men who had offered her protection if she agreed to appear before a federal grand jury. It wasn't just the dark jeans and worn leather jacket he was wearing either. It was something much more elusive, something uncompromising in his stance and in the hard lines of a face that could only be described as experienced and utterly masculine. Leigh couldn't have found words for it if she'd tried, but she also couldn't shake the feeling that there was more maverick than public servant in the man.

On the other hand, he didn't look like her idea of hired muscle either, and she found herself succumbing to a fierce desire to believe he was not here to deliver a very physical lecture on the wisdom of settling your debts in a timely fashion. She exhaled deeply and, as if that were some sort of signal, he returned the I.D. to his back pocket.

"All right, Mr. Cutter," she said in an attempt to sound calm and agreeable, "you're a federal agent. You still haven't told me why you're here."

"To protect you."

The answer was uttered in a voice that was deep, faintly gruff, and strangely unemotional. The lingering traces of a southwestern drawl did nothing to soften the implacable intent in those three little words.

"From whom?"

His steely gray eyes shot her an impatient look. "Your friend DeMarco for starters."

Just the name had the power to make Leigh blanch. "He's not a friend of mine."

"Just your friendly neighborhood loanshark, huh?"

"I didn't know he—" She broke off abruptly, remembering the vivid warning Vinnie Gilman had issued when she told him she planned to cooperate with the federal agents. "I'm going to tell you the same thing I told your two cohorts a few days ago. I don't know any Eddie DeMarco, and I don't know anything that would be of interest to a grand jury."

Nothing about his hard expression altered except for the fleeting glint in his eyes that suggested to Leigh that her attempt to throw up a smokescreen had failed.

"Come off it, lady," he urged softly. "A few minutes ago you were talking a blue streak about beatings and paybacks and documents implicating a man you now claim you don't even know."

Leigh nervously smoothed the bottom of her pale pink sweater over the curve of her hips. "So I was a little rattled. I think it's an understandable reaction when you consider that I'm here alone and a strange man had just planted his foot in the doorway and insisted he had to talk to me."

"And what rattled you back in the restaurant?"

"You!" she snapped, trying to hide the fact that his quiet attempt at intimidation was working.

"How? I didn't say a word to you."

"You didn't have to. It was the way you were looking at me." She hesitated, remembering how she'd first felt the power of his gaze, then turned and been momentarily stunned by the sheer intensity of it. Now, as then, she felt an inexplicable sense of alarm, as if she were confronting a natural predator, one who was wily and unpredictable. The image of a dark, sleek panther flashed before her.

"Men look at women all the time," he pointed out, a shade of amusement in his laconic drawl.

"Not that way," Leigh sneered. "I could tell there was something deeper than purely masculine interest in that look."

"Lady, there *is* nothing deeper than purely masculine interest."

"What's that supposed to mean?"

He frowned, carving tiny fans of lines around his eyes. He appeared as perplexed as she was by the nature of his retort.

"Nothing," he said finally with a shrug that was distinctly final. "Now why don't you go put on a pot of coffee while I show myself around. Then we'll talk."

Leigh blinked in disbelief. "What do you think this is—an open house? I am not your maid, I don't feel like talking, and—although this may be difficult for a government type like yourself to comprehend—I do have rights."

"None that I'm particularly interested in at the moment—other than your right not to become a victim in a power play I suspect you don't even understand."

His mouth had twisted into a smile. It was a trifle sardonic, but he seemed more comfortable with it than with the courteous ones he'd attempted up till now. To Leigh, he still looked about as friendly and approachable as a hungry Doberman. It probably had something to do with that black beard, she decided. She hated beards.

"And just for the record," he continued, "I wasn't demanding coffee; I was requesting it. And I want to look around because I feel more comfortable in a situation like this when I know where all the doors and windows are. And if you want to know more than that, put on the coffee and we'll talk."

Before Leigh could respond, he brushed past her on the landing and started determinedly down the stairs to the lower level, where the family room and garage were located.

"A situation like what?" she finally thought to shout after him. It almost seemed as if a chuckle floated back to her, but Leigh quickly dismissed the idea. She doubted that a man who couldn't smile had the capacity to do something as carefree as laugh. "And you did too demand it."

He had demanded it, and it rankled Leigh to be ordered about by a man she didn't know or want to know. Still, she trudged up the short flight of stairs to her sister's cheery yellow and white kitchen and began measuring coffee into the pot. As it started hissing and brewing, she began to wonder about the extent of all those rights she'd so confidently claimed. Cutter had said he was here to protect her. While that had a welcome ring to it, she wondered if he had the authority to force his protection on her against her will. She could still recall Vinnie saying that the only thing DeMarco despised more than a welsher was one who had a big mouth. And she vividly recalled the anecdotes he'd used to illustrate how harshly such individuals were dealt with.

Somehow, instinctively, she knew that Mitch Cutter had what it would take to protect her from DeMarco's wrath. But for how long? Until the grand jury hearing? Until DeMarco was tried and convicted? Until he was paroled for good behavior after God knew how short a time? She slammed two of her sister's good mottled-jade mugs onto the counter with alarming force, then quickly checked for chips or cracks. There weren't any—in the mugs *or* in her resolve to keep her mouth shut and extricate herself from this mess on her own, as quickly and safely as possible.

She'd come up here to sort out her thoughts and decide on a plan of action, and she had done that. The appearance of Mitch Cutter wasn't going to alter her plans one iota; it simply gave her a chance to tell these federal investigators once and for all that she had nothing to say. Then, somehow, she would have to convince DeMarco that she was responsible only for three thousand dollars of the outlandish loan Vinnie had secured in both their names. With any luck, she would be able to repay that amount, plus interest, before the end of the summer. If he refused to wait that long, well, she'd just have to ask her sister, Debby, and brother-in-law, Mike, to bail her out—and hope that they didn't forget they were the ones who'd started this nightmarish ball rolling by urging her to open the inn in the first place.

By the time her stone-faced, unwanted protector had

come upstairs, inspected the three bedrooms, bath, living, and dining rooms, and joined her in the kitchen, the coffee was ready. And so was Leigh.

"Thank you," he said as she handed him one of the oversized mugs, taking a cautious sip without bothering with the cream or sugar she'd set out.

Leigh lightened her own coffee and climbed onto one of the stools near the butcher-block counter.

"You might as well sit down," she invited with all the hospitality she could manage.

"Thanks."

His scintillating conversational powers inspired her to respond in kind. "So talk."

"Talk?"

"That was the deal: I was to make the coffee, and you were to do the talking."

He almost smiled, that same awkward slant of his lips he seemed to have trouble maintaining. "The house is pretty tight. The lock on one of the windows at the back of the garage is missing though. I secured it temporarily with a board, but it's nothing anyone with a little know-how and determination couldn't knock loose."

"Fascinating. But is all this official diligence really necessary?"

He looked at her oddly. "You tell me, lady. You're the one who picked this for a hiding place. I should think you would have checked for little details like broken locks."

"I did not come here to hide," Leigh countered hotly. She refused to admit that even to herself, lest the inherent danger in this situation push her to the brink of cardiac arrest. "I came here to think, to sort things out."

"Things like how you're going to pay back DeMarco?

And whether or not it's worth it to testify against him at the grand jury hearing? And whether he'd be more angry to learn you'd opened your mouth or that you couldn't come up with the cash?"

"But I will come up with it!" she exclaimed, then broke off, irritated with him and herself.

"In time?"

"I told you before, I don't have anything to say about any of this."

He shrugged and stared into his empty mug. "Fine. I only offered to talk it over to soothe your nerves. Myself, I like things quiet."

Leigh pushed her still full mug away and stood; she had no intention of offering him a refill.

"Thank you for stopping by and checking on me," she said, adding tartly, "it's reassuring to know your agency is so concerned about my well-being. Now if you like, I'll show you to the door."

The "if you like" had been purely rhetorical. When he didn't respond in a similarly polite manner by following her lead, but remained sitting, staring at her with that odd expression again, Leigh turned and faced him with an exasperated sigh.

"The door," she prompted.

"I've already checked it out."

"I remember. I was offering to show *you* out."

"That's out of the question," he responded with a quiet authority that made the hairs along the back of Leigh's neck bristle with her heart-sinking premonition.

"What do you mean it's out of the question?"

"Just what I said. I've already explained to you that I'm here to protect you."

"And I explained to you that I don't need protection."

He inclined his head, either oblivious or immune to the icy chill in her tone. "My superiors obviously think otherwise."

"That's their problem."

"Actually, I have a feeling it just became mine."

The indulgent amusement suggested by the thoughtful way he stroked his beard and the almost imperceptible twitch at one corner of his lips only compounded her annoyance.

"Well, you are hereby relieved of the problem. You've done your duty by coming here and offering your protection, and I am graciously declining."

The twitch intensified maddeningly. "I'm afraid you can't do that."

"Of course I can. It's my decision whether or not I want to be protected."

"Not in this case. I'm afraid the only decision you get to make is whether we do it the easy way or the hard way."

"Meaning what?"

"Meaning you can make life a lot easier—and more pleasant—for both of us by simply accepting the fact that I'm going to be your shadow until we get this all straightened out."

"There's nothing to straighten out."

"Right, I know. You don't have anything to say to the grand jury investigators."

"That's right."

"And you also don't have the money you owe DeMarco."

"I told you—"

He cut short her angry denial by lifting his hand, long fingers outstretched. "Okay, you don't owe him any money. But, hypothetically, just between the two of us, if you did owe him anything, would you be able to pay it back on his terms—like immediately?"

Leigh held her breath for several seconds before releasing it in a defeated rush. What difference did it make if she admitted that much to him, here, with no witnesses? She'd already blundered royally at the door when she mistook him for one of DeMarco's errand boys.

"All right, *hypothetically,* no. I don't have the money."

He nodded grimly. "Which explains why you need my protection."

Leigh found his emphasis on the word *my* puzzling and vaguely unsettling. "Except I get the feeling you're not here so much to protect me as to persuade me—coerce me—into testifying against DeMarco."

"Not at all. I don't know enough about this whole thing yet to decide what you should do."

Leigh's eyes widened in surprise that quickly gave way to a mingling of contempt and grudging admiration. "Very clever. Next I suppose you're going to suggest I tell you all about it so you can make a decision—for my own good of course."

"That would be the next logical step."

"And a very stupid one for me. For all I know, you're wearing one of those hidden tape recorders, or a bug."

"A bug?" Something flashed like silver in his steely gray eyes. "Do you by any chance watch an inordinate amount of television detective shows?"

"Enough to know you could be luring me into saying things I don't want to say and recording every word."

He rose and in one long stride moved to where she stood in the doorway. "Frisk me."

"What?"

"Frisk me. Don't tell me a woman with your broad knowledge of law enforcement techniques doesn't understand the term."

"I understand!" she snapped, crossing her arms in front of her. "I just don't know what that would prove."

"That I'm not wearing any sort of device for one thing, and that I'm willing to go to whatever lengths it takes to convince you I'm here for one reason only: to see that nothing happens to you while you're sorting things out."

Leigh mulled that over. She did not want him here, but short of bodily throwing him out—a ludicrous notion—she wasn't quite sure how to dislodge Mitch Cutter from the premises. He seemed like the sort who took his work very seriously, and something about the earnest determination in his eyes when he spoke about protecting her suggested he consider this a mission of the highest order. Until she could figure out how to get rid of him, it would be vastly reassuring to know that every word she uttered, every slip she made, wasn't going to be used against her sometime in the future.

"Take off your jacket," she ordered in a clipped tone.

He slowly shrugged it from his shoulders and began to toss it onto the stool behind him.

"Uh-uh, I'll check that first," she announced with a smug lilt in her tone.

He obligingly handed it over and watched with a little smugness of his own as she spread it out on the counter and patted it all over without detecting a single suspicious bump or mound. Only when she began to rifle through his pockets did he display even a flicker of discomfiture. When she reached the inside pocket, Leigh tugged out the folded white envelope she found there and shook the contents onto the table. Frowning, she quickly scanned the list of her friends' names and addresses and then focused on the well-worn photograph.

"How . . . ?" she began, looking up at him with a thoroughly perplexed expression. "Where did you get this?"

"I was given the picture when I was sent to look for you. To be sure I'd recognize you."

"But Vinnie took this picture this past fall. Did he give it to your agency?"

"I'm not sure."

"He had to have. Does that mean he's decided to cooperate with the investigation?"

He shook his head. "I don't know the answer to that."

Leigh tossed the picture down, angry with Cutter's unresponsiveness and more confused than ever now that it seemed that Vinnie, who'd so urgently advised her to banish the foolhardy notion of cooperating with the federal investigators, had done exactly the opposite. Had he wanted them to find her? Was this his way of telling her she should comply with their requests after all? And if it was, how could she trust him after the scheming way he'd involved her in all this to begin with? She couldn't—any more than she could trust the man watching her with gray eyes that never wavered, making her feel stripped down to her soul.

"You're not sure?" she mimicked frostily. "You don't know? Who are you—some rookie they sent up here to handle the irksome details?"

"Rookie or not," he replied without a trace of the irritation Leigh would have found so satisfying, "I'm capable of handling what needs to be done here."

"Namely affording me protection?"

He nodded. "Now, if you've satisfied yourself that I'm not hiding anything else, may I pour myself another cup of coffee?"

"I'm not satisfied."

"Then see to it, woman," he ordered, lifting his arms away from his sides. "I'm tired and thirsty."

It took Leigh two steps to reach him and another six heartbeats before she realized she didn't have the faintest idea of how to go about frisking him without becoming more familiar with his tall, uncompromisingly masculine body than she had any desire to be. Until this moment, she had seen him alternately as a cause for fear, irritation, and frustration. Suddenly she was seeing him as a man first and foremost, and for some reason that was infinitely more unsettling.

Looking for a safe place to begin, she dropped her dismayed eyes to his boots and ran them back up slowly until they collided with the honest-to-goodness smile plastered on his face.

"Would you like me to talk you through it this first time, honey?" he inquired pointedly.

Lord, the man was arrogant! No, not exactly arrogant, she amended quickly. Arrogance in a man could almost be chuckled over and so dismissed. The quality exuded by Mitch Cutter's eloquently arched brows and suddenly laughing eyes was something much more subtle and un-affected—and that, Leigh realized glumly, made it a force to be reckoned with.

"Thanks," she replied curtly, "but I'm sure I can find the way by myself."

"I can hardly wait."

Ignoring the dry rejoinder, Leigh determinedly lifted her hands to his hair. She wasn't sure if an electronic bug could be concealed there, but she wasn't sure it couldn't be either, and she had no intention of making a clumsy oversight. The idea that if she did, each syllable she uttered would be interpreted and dissected by some unknown investigator was bad enough; the thought of facing the glint of smug triumph her error would likely inspire in those gray eyes was loathsome. It was enough to send her fingers fluttering over him in spite of her nervousness.

She feathered through his thick, nearly black hair, following the swept-back path it formed over his ears to where it brushed the collar of his blue chambray shirt in back. Then she patted her way along the considerable breadth of his shoulders and the arms he held so docilely suspended. Next, she surveyed the hard terrain of his chest, vividly aware through the soft cotton of his shirt that he was wearing nothing beneath it, and that his chest was well-muscled and nearly as covered with the proof of his virility as his chin was.

Reaching around, she began to check out his back. She was deeply engrossed in a silent debate about whether or not to abandon the search at his waist, when a rush of warm, coffee-scented breath tickled her temple, alerting her to the fact that she was now standing very close to him—as close as in a lovers' embrace. Close enough, she thought, jerking back, for him to deduce that she wasn't wearing anything beneath her sweater either.

"Turn around," she commanded after glancing up to find his expression deceptively, infuriatingly bland.

The smile was all in his eyes now . . . and in his quiet, obliging, "Whatever you say, ma'am."

She resumed her task with renewed determination, her fingers coasting unerringly and relentlessly over the stiff denim that covered his lean hips—front and back— and long, muscular legs. When she finally stood once more, her cheeks were as pink as her mohair sweater, and she was the somewhat flustered possessor of the indisputable knowledge that Mitch Cutter was, first and foremost, a man.

"Will you please take off your boots?" she asked in a tone that made the polite request a command.

Mitch raised his eyebrows again, but he sat and began tugging them off. "You are thorough."

"I can't afford not to be."

She ran her hands lightly over his sock-clad feet and inside the boots, still having little idea of precisely what she should be looking for but satisfied that she'd done her best to insure her own security.

"Find anything interesting?" he asked when she dropped the boots at his feet and retreated to the other side of the kitchen.

Something in his too-neutral tone made Leigh meet his glittering gray gaze head-on and retort, "Not in the least."

He chuckled at that. The short, gravelly sound drifted over to her as he bent to put his boots on, surprising her and making her think the man might not be quite the government-programmed robot he seemed.

"Well, then," he drawled, "now that we've got everything else settled, do you think I could have another cup of coffee?"

"You can have more coffee," Leigh replied, carrying the pot over to refill his mug. "But we definitely have not got everything settled. All I know is that you're here to protect me and that you don't plan on leaving any time soon." She watched him sip his coffee, obviously at peace with that assessment of their situation. "I'd like to know exactly what your notion of protecting me entails."

He smoothed the side of his beard with his outstretched fingers. "I plan to do whatever is necessary to see that nothing happens to you."

"For how long?"

A crease appeared between his dark brows, suggesting a degree of impatience with what he obviously thought were stupid questions. "For however long it takes, of course."

"You mean for as long as I remain here at my sister's?"

"I mean just what I said: for as long as it takes."

"What if I return home to Jamestown?"

"We'll cross that bridge when we come to it."

"Who we? You and I? Or your all-powerful superiors?"

"I was speaking euphemistically. I should have said *I'll* cross that bridge when we come to it."

"You expect me to believe that you make your own decisions in these matters?"

"That would be extremely wise on your part, but I really don't expect you to believe anything—except that, want it or not, I am going to see you safely through this mess you've gotten yourself into."

Leigh mulled that over for a minute, looking for a vulnerable spot to start chinking away at his position. There wasn't one. "I take it you plan to stay here with me? Day *and* night?"

An indulgent smile came to life on his lips. "I'd find it sort of hard to keep an eye on you from a motel twenty miles away. I'm good, Ms. Bramwell, but I'm not that good."

"Doesn't our staying here together strike you as a little . . . improper? I mean, we hardly know each other."

"Why, Ms. Bramwell, what could possibly happen? As you just pointed out, we hardly know each other."

He delivered the comeback in that same damn emotionless tone, leaving Leigh to wonder if he was laughing at her or baiting her or offering sincere reassurance.

At a loss for how else to respond, she snapped, "And will you please stop calling me Ms. Bramwell in that phony respectful way? I feel as if I'm back in high school being lectured for not doing my homework."

"What would you prefer I call you?"

"Leigh, I suppose," she sighed.

She could tell from the flicker of satisfaction in his eyes that he interpreted that as tantamount to a surrender. Well, he could go ahead and think that. It just might make him drop his guard for a while, and that could only help her cause, because Leigh was in no way prepared to surrender so easily.

"Okay, Leigh," he said, his deep voice turning her name into an odd caress that drew her gaze back to his. "You might as well call me Mitch. I have a feeling it's more flattering than what you'd like to call me about now."

"It's nothing personal," she admitted glumly. "I know you're just doing your job."

"That's one way of looking at it." Before she could ask what other way there was, he continued, "Now, do you mind if I ask you a question?" Predictably, he didn't wait for her permission before asking it. "Are you wearing some sort of strange, sweet perfume?"

"If I was I'd hardly admit it now, after that flattering description. Really, strange and sweet?"

"Right." He sniffed the air. "Sort of like coconut."

"Coconut? Oh no!"

Leigh lurched off the stool and snatched the quilted mitts from the counter near the stove. In less than ten seconds she had the oven door open and a casserole full of a bubbling creamy substance in her hands.

"It didn't burn," she announced.

"What a relief," Mitch added, echoing her pleased tone. "What is it?"

"Coconut chicken. At least that's the name in English. Technically it's called *Oopa . . . Orpa . . .*"

"Opar ajam?" he supplied helpfully as she stumbled over the unfamiliar words.

Leigh looked up at him in amazement. "That's it. How did you know that?"

Mitch shrugged. "I spent some time in Southeast Asia a while back."

"Vietnam?"

"Somewhere near there."

"Were you in the military?" she pressed in spite of the shuttered look in his eyes.

"More or less. I was part of a special unit operating in that area for a while. The important question is, how did you learn to make *opar ajam?*"

"Oh, I took a course in Southeast Asian cuisine a while back," she responded, proceeding to stir the dish while executing a credible rendition of his evasive shrug.

"Isn't that a rather unusual cooking course to take?"

"Not for me. I'm working my way through the entire curriculum of the local high school's adult special interest courses."

"And you're already up to the S's? What other interesting talents do you possess?"

Leigh detected a note of genuine interest in his question, and she saw it reflected in his eyes when she turned to face him. It kept her from replying as flippantly as she'd intended to.

"I'm not quite up to the S's," she admitted, "because I'm not going about this in any particular order. But I have had a smattering of needlepoint, cooking with herbs, yoga, creative writing, assertiveness training, to name just a few."

"An impressive cross section," he pronounced solemnly. "Any particular reason for this undertaking?"

This time Leigh's shrug was thoroughly her own, a little uncertain, a little reluctant. "Not really. I was so obsessed with taking all the sensible, required courses while I was in college that I never had time for any of the fun ones. Now I do."

"Cooking Southeast Asian dishes is your idea of fun?"

Again Leigh found herself responding to the note of sincerity in his question. "I haven't decided yet. This was my first attempt outside of class."

His smile came and went in a flash, giving way to a concerned frown that tipped the edges of his firm lips downward and returned the tempered steel to his gaze. "That's a pretty big dish. Were you expecting someone else?"

"No—least of all you."

"Are you trying to tell me you were planning to eat all that yourself?"

"Not that it's any of your business, but I wasn't planning to eat it at all. I was just going to let it cool and stick it into the freezer for my sister's family." When he continued to look at her with an expression of disbelief, she added irritably, "Some people pace or eat when they're nervous. I cook."

"You have no reason to be nervous now that I'm here."

There was something dark and unyielding in his tone, and Leigh wasn't sure whether she should be feeling reassured or alarmed. She forced a small laugh to cover her confusion. "That's too bad, because I've already bought the ingredients for three more recipes I want to try out."

His frown disappeared slowly, usurped by a look of vague disappointment that drifted from her to the casserole she'd placed on the stove. "Were you serious about not planning to eat *any* of that?"

Leigh eyed him pointedly. "Cutter, you may be good, but you're not very subtle." Sighing, she added, "But I suppose as long as you're here and it's ready, you might as well enjoy it."

He did, with a quiet enthusiasm that stroked Leigh's ego and warmed her heart in a way she knew she shouldn't permit. She even softened enough to unwrap the deluxe sour cream chocolate cake she had ready for the freezer and offer him a piece.. He accepted it with a slightly startled eagerness that stuck in her mind simply because it hinted at vulnerability in a man she was certain didn't know the meaning of the word.

Their dinnertime conversation was minimal and prudently neutral. Mitch Cutter seemed content to skim over whatever inconsequential topic arose, and that made Leigh even more wary. She was still sure that part of his job was to persuade her to cooperate with the official investigation into DeMarco's affairs, but obviously his approach was not going to be as straightforward as his colleagues' had been. Leigh had the impression that he was observing her carefully, weighing her every move and response, looking for chinks in *her* armor.

More certain than ever that she couldn't afford to live side by side with the man as he ferreted out her weaknesses, she rushed him out of the kitchen the minute he finished his dessert, insisting that she preferred to do the dishes alone. He acquiesced with such ease that she found herself wondering if he'd ever once slung a dishcloth in the thirty-five-or-so years he appeared to have been on this earth. That led quite naturally into wondering if he could possibly be married. She quickly dismissed the idea with a derisive shake of her head. Married to his job, perhaps, or to his Jeep, or something else as cold and emotionless as he was, but not to a woman. She'd wager there was too much of the loner in Cutter to ever move him to want or need any woman enough to marry her. For some reason that notion stirred some intrinsically feminine response deep in Leigh. A man like that would certainly present an exciting challenge.

But not for her, she admitted, placing the final glass into the dishwasher and turning it on. She liked her challenges in nice, easily digested doses. And she'd reaffirmed during the past couple of weeks that she didn't like taking risks at all. That's why she had to handle this thing with DeMarco her way. That was also why she was going to have to leave Mitch Cutter if he wouldn't leave her alone.

Feigning overwhelming fatigue, she escaped to her room as soon after the evening news as seemed credible, first graciously offering to show him where he could put the small leather overnight bag he'd brought in from the car. To her dismay, Mitch announced that he'd already decided to sleep in the smallest of the three bedrooms, her nephew Michael's, because it was right at the top of the stairs, where he could hear anything that moved. It was for exactly the same reason that Leigh had planned to stick him in her niece Kristen's room tucked away at the far end of the hall.

For the next three hours she lay on her bed, fully dressed, trying to read while her mind raced again and again over the plan she'd concocted. When she'd first decided to escape, she'd felt a twinge of remorse over leaving a perfect stranger alone in her sister's house, but she forced herself to consider the unsavory alternative.

Besides, he was a government employee. That should count for something.

Finally, sometime after ten, she heard the unmistakable sounds of her watchdog slipping into bed, and she allowed another forty-five minutes for him to fall asleep before slipping out of hers. Grabbing a small tote bag she'd stuffed with enough clothes to see her through two or three days, she began to make her way down the hall. All of a sudden the short walk to the staircase seemed miles long—miles of some of the most nerve-racking terrain Leigh had ever traveled.

In a burst of paranoia, she wondered if her bare feet were making any noise as they padded at a snail's pace along the plush carpet. It was hard for her to tell over the internal ruckus created by her pounding heart and the blood roaring through her head. Lord, she wasn't cut out for this life of stealth. And to think she'd once longed to be Nancy Drew. She was still feeling her way along the wall, judging herself to be somewhere opposite the door to Mitch's room, when a deep, infinitely controlled voice pierced the black silence around her.

"Leigh."

She was holding her breath, trying to determine if there had been the slightest hint of uncertainty in his tone, when he spoke again and confirmed her gut sensation that there had not been.

"Leigh, I just thought I'd save you a long, cold walk down to the garage. When I checked in there earlier, I took the precaution of disconnecting the battery cable in your car."

The words, delivered in that gritty, unemotional voice, transformed whatever trepidation she had been feeling into pure, unadulterated fury. Flinging away her boots and tote bag, she charged into his room, switching on the light with a jerky motion.

"How dare you?" she demanded, feeling beaten and outsmarted and incensed and at a loss for words violent enough to express her emotions to the man still sprawled on the single bed.

"It wasn't all that daring," he returned laconically. "Disconnecting a battery cable is pretty simple stuff."

She glared at him. "Then what makes you so sure I won't just go and reconnect it?"

"I gambled that you wouldn't know how," he admitted. "If it turns out you've also taken a course in basic auto repair, then I suppose I'll have to find a less gentle way of stopping you."

"Why you smug, arrogant . . . bastard!"

The words seemed to slide right off him, not causing so much as a muscle twitch in his calm expression. In desperation, Leigh grabbed the plastic robot adorning her nephew's dresser and hurled it at him. She was as surprised as Mitch when the head popped off on contact, spilling an avalanche of pennies all over him. That didn't, however, stop her from reaching for the small armored tank that had been sitting next to the robot.

"Don't even consider it," Mitch growled.

At last there was some emotion in his soft voice. But standing there, trapped in his steely gaze, Leigh wasn't sure if she was glad or sorry she'd provoked it. Slowly, she let her hand drop back to her side.

Mitch shifted in the bed, propping himself up on one elbow and sending pennies cascading everywhere in the process. "Listen, Leigh, I know this has been a long, hard day for you, too, but I'm very tired, and I'm in no mood to lie here and let you use me for target practice."

"You're right," she agreed with a syrupy smile, "it's

a waste of time... especially when I'd much rather be using a gun."

"I'm sure you would. But as long as you don't have one handy, go back to bed."

"I don't have to take orders from you."

"No, but if you're smart you will."

"Go to hell."

"I'd rather just go to sleep. Now, please turn off the light and go back to your own room or else I'm going to get out of this bed and carry you back there myself. And I promise you, Leigh, you won't like it if I do."

It must have been temporary insanity brought on by anxiety, she decided later. With uncharacteristic recklessness, she ignored the frantic clamoring of her common sense telling her to retreat. She forced herself to stand there and face him with the most defiant expression she could manage as she drawled, "I'm not afraid of you."

Mitch sighed, and a glint of something that could have been amusement flashed in his eyes.

"I wasn't suggesting you should be," he said, dropping his gaze briefly and eloquently to his bare chest before leveling it at her once more. "I was simply trying to warn you that I don't wear pajama *bottoms* either."

Chapter Three

BEFORE LEIGH COULD rethink her ill-timed bravado, he was out of the bed and lunging across the room, looking irritated, determined, and as naked as threatened.

At the unadorned sight of the lean masculine planes and hard-muscled ridges her fingers had already become acquainted with, her eyes first opened wide then squeezed shut in a face that was rapidly turning from pale to scarlet.

"Wait!" she croaked. "I—"

A quick, instinctive step backward brought her up against the solid wood doorframe just as his arms reached out to grab her, hauling her unceremoniously over his equally solid shoulder.

She kept her eyes fixed on the carpet as he sauntered— sauntered! she thought, enraged anew—back down the hall to the room she was using.

"You have no right—"

"The hell I don't," he cut her off. "I warned you."

"Some warning. You didn't even give me a chance to move."

"Lady, I gave you a whole five seconds more of a chance than I would have given anyone else."

"Thank you so much," she drawled snidely. "Why was I singled out for such special treatment?"

"I wish to hell I knew," he replied, lowering his shoulder to dump her in the center of the bed.

Straightening, he stood there looking down at her with an expression Leigh couldn't quite figure out. He no longer looked irritated, and she breathed a cowardly sigh of relief. He also didn't look amused, which was a relief in a different sort of way. He looked . . . thoughtful. She anchored her gaze on his face and tried to figure out what he was thinking, primarily to avoid letting herself contemplate the sheer awkwardness of having to lie there being scrutinized by a naked man.

"Are you done now?" she inquired finally, striving for a withering tone.

He obviously did not wither easily. "That all depends," he drawled. "Are *you* done now?"

"Do you mean am I just going to throw in the towel and admit you beat me hands down? Am I going to let you bully me and order me around in my own sister's home? Am I going to docilely accept your presence here after I've made it abundantly clear you are not wanted?" She paused, savoring the wariness that narrowed his eyes and injected a hint of tension into his casual stance, before shrugging and saying with sweet compliance, "Of course I'm done."

He raked his fingers through his hair in a way Leigh found satisfyingly exasperated before finally announcing, "All right then, take off your jacket."

"As soon as you get out of here and give me some privacy."

"You forfeited your right to privacy when you tried to bolt." He held out his hand and repeated quietly, "Your jacket, Leigh."

It was a small thing, this calm way he had of issuing orders as if he were born to command and she to respond, but it provoked in Leigh a streak of rebelliousness she was shocked to discover. Without taking the time to wonder why, after twenty-seven years of lying dormant, that rebelliousness should suddenly flare to life within hours of her meeting this man, or why it seemed so desperately important not to surrender to him even one more inch, she crossed her arms and met his flinty gaze head on.

"I said I'll take it off after you leave."

"That's impossible," he countered smoothly, "because I'm not leaving until you hand it over. I don't think you're desperate enough to make a run for it without a jacket in this weather."

"Don't bet on it," she muttered under her breath. Then she lifted her chin to toss him a triumphant smile that belied the uneasiness mushrooming inside. "At any rate, it looks like a stalemate."

"Not by a long shot, honey."

Too quickly for her to react, much less resist, his hands shot out and jerked her arms open, then grasped the pull of her zipper and wrenched it down. By the time Leigh started to struggle, he'd dropped to his knees on the bed and was leaning over her, methodically working the jacket off her shoulders.

Instantly, she brought her arms up and discovered that the only part of him she could get a grip on was his upper arms. They felt like granite beneath her grasping fingers, the muscles there flexed and unyielding. In desperation she curled her fingers and dug them into his flesh, her only reward the almost imperceptible clenching of his teeth. He did not respond in kind, however. His efforts at stripping off her jacket remained controlled, almost grimly gentle.

That only struck Leigh as further evidence of his smug condescension—as if she weren't worthy of anger or the expenditure of any real effort—and sent a wave of frustration crashing over her. Riding its crest, she began to fight in earnest, her movements making up in spirit what they lacked in skill and coordination.

Without relinquishing his hold on her parka, Mitch paused to gape at her in amazement, emitting a gruff sound of surprise that was quickly followed by a long, low chuckle of amusement. The gravelly laugh spurred Leigh on. She raked her fingernails across his chest, then shoved at it with all her ineffectual might, her legs thrashing wildly as she struggled to break his hold. She wasn't even aware that she'd brought her knee up and was holding it strategically poised, making of it a lethal weapon if aimed correctly, until Mitch forced it roughly back to the mattress and anchored it there with his own much stronger leg.

"Oh no, you don't," he grunted, shifting his weight fully on top of her, driving home to Leigh in less than an instant what a foolish, ridiculous farce her show of resistance had been. "Who'd ever have thought you'd turn into a fighter? And such a dirty one at that?"

She stared up at him, fully cognizant of what he thought she'd been trying to do to him, and humiliated herself further by blushing. "I didn't . . ." she began awkwardly. "I mean, I wasn't trying . . ."

"Shhh." His deep voice held a soft, soothing note she hadn't expected. "You don't have to explain. I wouldn't have blamed you if you *had* managed to knee me."

He lowered one hand and gently stroked the curve of her cheek, easily keeping her arms uselessly entwined in the jacket above her head with the other. His gaze drifted over her face with a searching intensity that was all wrong. He should be angry, Leigh thought, or treating her with that offhand arrogance he managed so effortlessly. Not with this unexpected tender interest, as if he'd stopped looking at her merely as his latest assignment and was suddenly seeing her as—as a woman! she realized on a new swell of panic.

She swallowed hard and felt her pulse, which had begun to slow to normal, start to race once more. At the same time, she could sense her breathing becoming ragged and shallow, as if she were struggling against him all over again. And each quick breath lifted her breasts into intimate contact with the broad, hair-roughened chest poised just above her. Leigh could feel the heat of his body right through her sweater, and lower, through the crisp denim covering her hips and legs. For the second time that day she was made intensely aware of him as a man.

Mitch seemed to be equally aware of her discomfiture, but if he guessed the reason, he did nothing to alleviate it.

Continuing his idle caress of her face, he spoke to her in a voice that was rough and touched with concern. "Poor angel. When you finally decide to stop running and fight, you end up fighting the wrong man. But you don't know that yet, do you, angel?"

"I don't want to know anything," Leigh stated, carefully averting her gaze until he tipped her face to bring it back to his. "I just want you to leave me alone. You can take the jacket," she added in a meek attempt to placate.

Mitch frowned at her. "What about what *I* want?"

"I don't care what you want," she whispered.

Tiny lines edged his eyes as he gazed down at her speculatively. "I could make you want the same thing," he threatened in a soft growl.

"How?" she demanded, frantic to resist this new menace in him. "By beating me into submission? Maybe you should be working for DeMarco after all; you seem to have all the right moves."

Something hard flickered in his dark eyes. "Don't ever say that again," he warned harshly. "I don't even want you to think it."

He looked torn between rage and anguish, and for an instant she thought he was going to slam out of the room. But he stayed, watching her with a black, tortured expression, making Leigh more sorry by the minute that she'd uttered the impulsive accusation in the first place. She was on the brink of delivering a grudging apology when he muttered a rough, "Oh, what the hell," and lowered his mouth to claim hers in a savage conquest, sealing the words deep in her throat.

It was a kiss like none Leigh had ever experienced—if *kiss* was the proper word. It was more an act of domination, overpowering, primitive, as devoid of emotion as everything else about the man. It was as if he'd set out to prove that in this, at least, he would not be defied.

His tongue stabbed at her lips, and when she refused to comply with that silent command, he used his teeth and his grip on her jaw to force her to yield. She opened her mouth with a small whimper as he swept inside, moving his tongue in rough, aggressive thrusts that had nothing to do with passion. Too shocked to fight, she lay paralyzed beneath him. Then, as suddenly as she had managed to provoke it, he brought his aggression under control. Leigh could feel the tension rippling through the strong body pressed to every inch of hers, could hear it in the ragged edge of his breathing.

Burying his face in her hair, he began to slide his fingers over her skin once more, coasting gently over her throat, soothing, cajoling. At first Leigh held herself in tight unresponsiveness, but gradually her muscles began to relax, responding to the tender touch her mind was determined to resist. As if he felt her tension melting, Mitch lifted his head to gaze down at her. It occurred to Leigh slowly that there was neither triumph nor satisfaction in his expression, just a shadow of remorse as he once more bent to touch her lips with his.

This kiss was as different from the first as silver from sand. This time he courted her senses with a gentle persuasiveness that made her forget she hated him. Even his beard, which had grated against her skin so roughly the last time, now seemed less offensive. In fact, it added a new, wildly masculine sensation to the unhurried kiss that Leigh found arousing in spite of herself. Would it feel as good brushing against other parts of her body? she wondered hazily as the movements of his tongue grew deeper and bolder.

With each damp stroke, each rhythmic twist of his body against hers, she became more aware of the hunger in him. It was primitive and exciting . . . and, she realized, as firmly under his control as all his other emotions. Again that untested feminine instinct deep inside flirted with the notion of what it would be like to be the woman who could unleash that hunger and satisfy it. An unexpected tremor ran through her at the thought, a tremor of pure desire, more searing than any she had ever felt.

It was as if all the fear and insanity of the past few days had battered down her natural defenses and ravaged her well-defined principles of what was proper and what was not. Certainly the Leigh Bramwell who lived her life quietly to the tune of a safe, sane set of rules would deem this wanton enjoyment of a perfect stranger—a perfectly *naked* stranger's kiss, no less—to be extremely foolhardy and inappropriate. But the woman who had come alive inside her, the woman whose senses were saturated by the strength and feel and scent of him, wished only that the kiss could go on forever.

When it didn't, when he pulled away from her with a tearing reluctance and a groan that came close to being an oath, she reached instinctively to draw him back, only to discover her hands were still bound in the sleeves of her jacket. Even before he had the twisted fabric loosened, sanity returned. With it came a suffocating wave of humiliation that left Leigh tongue-tied and silent as he stood and made a last, lingering sweep across her swollen bottom lip with his thumb.

"Good night, Leigh. And this time stay put," he added solemnly as he turned and pulled the door shut behind him on his way out.

He didn't take the jacket. He didn't have to. It was clear who had won.

Once she was certain he'd returned to his room, Leigh forced herself to get up and change into a flannel nightgown, as if nothing extraordinary had just happened and life would now proceed as normal. Entering the bathroom off the master bedroom, she went through the motions of brushing her teeth and washing her face without once looking herself in the eye in the mirror. Finally, she climbed back into bed feeling anything *but* normal.

She felt foolish and confused and more than a little anxious about what the morning would bring. In all likelihood the kiss had not been as earthshattering or out of the ordinary for Mitch as it had been for her. It had started in angry retaliation, then probably progressed as no more than an impetuous attempt to add some spice to a drudge assignment. And she'd responded like such a mindless simp that he would no doubt continue trying to amuse himself at her expense in the days ahead. The question was, how would she react the next time?

If forewarned was forearmed, then she was ready for him. She knew now what a powerful force his passion could be, even as tightly reined as it had been tonight. But she also knew that the real danger lay not in him, but in herself—in the power he had to ignite the passion in *her*. For a moment as she lay in his arms she had been a different woman, a woman seething with feelings and yearnings she didn't recognize. She had no doubt the real Leigh Bramwell could withstand his potent brand of sensuality, but she wasn't at all sure how to go about controlling this newly discovered passionate woman inside.

She woke before six the next morning and climbed out of bed armed with only a sketchy battle plan. Getting rid of him was obviously out of the question; escaping was only slightly less impossible. No, it seemed she was stuck with Mitch Cutter, at least until she decided to cooperate with his agency or came up with a way to convince them she wasn't hiding anything. In view of their persistence in hounding her, that seemed increasingly improbable, and as she wasn't yet ready to take the risk of cooperating, she was stuck.

The safest approach seemed to be to accept the situation and treat her . . . her bodyguard with a dignified, restrained cordiality. Fervent outbursts like last night's were only likely to incite the sort of passionate response—from the stranger without and within—that she was determined to avoid.

Pulling on a clean pair of jeans and a tailored shirt made of soft yellow flannel, she strode toward the kitchen to enjoy a solitary cup of coffee before facing the challenge ahead. How did one go about making friends with a watchdog? she wondered, stepping into the kitchen to discover she wasn't even to be allowed the luxury of a few moments alone to plot strategy.

Mitch was already up, standing in the adjoining dining room by the sliding glass doors that led to the deck, a cup of coffee in his hand. Dressed in jeans and a navy blue shirt, he added fresh ballast to the image of a dark, sleek panther that was never far from her mind when he was around.

At the sound of her footsteps on the kitchen's tile floor, he turned from surveying the pink glow of dawn playing across the snow outside and moved to the archway between the two rooms.

"Good morning, Leigh."

She kept her gaze glued to the coffeepot in her hand, determined not to spill it all over the counter and reveal how nervous he made her. "Morning. You're certainly up early."

Out of the corner of her eye she caught his look of surprise at the forced cheeriness in her voice. He'd obviously expected something different from her this morning, and it buoyed Leigh's confidence to be able to throw him off-balance even briefly.

"I've been up most of the night. I never sleep well in a strange place," he added with a shrug.

"Homesick?" she countered in an attempt at levity. The idea of this strong, fiercely self-controlled man suffering anything as touching as homesickness was laughable. Only Mitch wasn't laughing. He wasn't even smiling.

"No. It wasn't that," he said simply.

"Oh, I see," she replied, trying once more, this time with a smile to tip him off that she was joking with him. "You're plagued by nightmares?"

"No."

She rolled her eyes, muttering, "Maybe you just missed your favorite teddy bear."

Mitch frowned. "Of course not. It's just that when I'm working I like to know what's going on at all times. I don't relax much."

"You also don't have much of a sense of humor," she informed him. "I was only teasing about the teddy bear and being homesick."

"Oh. Now I get it." He attempted a smile. "I guess I don't have much of a sense of humor at that. But then, I've never had much cause to develop one."

Leigh stared at him in disbelief over the rim of her cup. "You don't have to develop a sense of humor, Mitch. It's just there, like your arms and legs."

"Then I guess I must be some sort of cripple. With me, it's not just there. I tend to take everything seriously and at face value." He hesitated, a private war going on in the steel-gray eyes fixed on her so intently. "Like last night," he said finally. "Were you teasing when you made that crack about my working for DeMarco?"

Leigh's teeth clamped over the edge of her bottom lip. "Not exactly. I was just mad because you're bigger and stronger than I am, and I knew I was losing."

"I want you to know I'm sorry."

"Why? It's not your fault you're bigger than I am."

"I meant about what happened after that."

The memory of his kiss burned to life in her mind. She licked her lips and tasted him, drew a breath and felt again the warmth of his chest pressing her into the mattress.

"Oh, that," she said, a tremble creeping into her voice, sabotaging her attempt to sound offhand. "Well, we were both upset. Look, can we just forget it ever happened?"

"I can try," he offered, the wry twist of his lips challenging Leigh's plan to fight passion with personality.

She forced down a surge of panic and smiled brightly. "Good. I think that would be best all around as long as we're going to be stuck with each other for a few days."

"I wanted to ask you about that. Have you given any thought to how much longer you might spend up here sorting things out?"

Leigh glanced up sharply from the bread she was feeding into the toaster. "Bored already?"

"I'll survive."

"Yes, I imagine you're very good at surviving."

"Which is lucky for you. Because you don't look— or fight—as if you could take care of yourself alone after dark in your own backyard."

Leigh's spine straightened. "I've managed all right on my own for twenty-seven years."

"I'd have to argue with that." He swung one of the heavy straight-back chairs out from the dining room table and straddled it backwards, his arms resting on the top. "If you could take care of yourself, you wouldn't be in the trouble you're in now. How did you manage to get yourself involved with DeMarco, honey?"

Leigh continued to butter her toast in silence.

"I have a feeling you wandered into this with your

eyes closed and didn't know what was really going on until you were in way over your head."

He sipped his coffee, obviously giving her a chance to agree or disagree if she wished. She didn't.

"You probably bit off more than you could chew with that hulk of an inn you're trying to whip into shape," he continued. "I can just imagine the plumbing and electrical contractors having a field day with a soft little thing like you. Did the final bills start exceeding the estimates? Forcing you to seek out some additional cash?"

The toast was gradually becoming a pile of greasy crumbs as Leigh continued to smear and stab at it with the knife. She knew she would choke if she tried to take a bite. Besides, if she moved to the table, she was certain Mitch would read in her face how frighteningly close to the truth he was getting with his casual hypotheses.

"But, creep that he is, it's not DeMarco's style to mislead the innocent," he continued in that same deep, lazy drawl. "It's to his advantage to make sure his, uh, clients understand the terms of the loan up front. Makes the collection process less messy. Which means there must be someone else involved in this with you. Someone who probably put you in contact with DeMarco in the first place. Who's Vinnie, Leigh?"

She stopped breathing, silently cursing herself for slipping up and mentioning Vinnie's name yesterday when she'd discovered that picture in Mitch's jacket pocket. If Mitch had to ask her who he was, then obviously Vinnie was not cooperating with their investigation. He must have gotten his hands on her picture some other way, but there wasn't time to speculate on that now. Mitch had shoved the chair out of his way and was pacing across the kitchen. He stopped just inches away, peering over her shoulder at the massacre on her plate.

"Were you planning to eat that? Or just grind it into oblivion?"

"I happen to like my toast well buttered."

"Then that piece should make you ecstatic," he remarked dryly, slipping the knife from her hand. When she immediately reached for a sponge to busy herself wiping crumbs from the counter, he grasped her by the shoulders and turned her to face him. "Who is he, Leigh?"

There was no laziness in his voice now, only a hard note of implacability that made Leigh quickly rule out open defiance as a form of response.

"He's a friend."

"How close a friend?"

She shrugged. To say he was a louse and no real friend at all would only raise more difficult questions.

Mitch's eyes narrowed in impatience. "All right, I'll be more specific—are you sleeping with him?" His hold on her shoulders tightened as she tried to pull away. "Answer me."

Leigh's eyes flashed. "I don't think it's any of your business whom I sleep with."

"It is if it's a misguided attempt to protect him that's stopping you from answering my questions." He raked her with a fierce look that was more possessive than professional. "And if you *have* been foolish enough to share your bed with a guy as sleazy as I suspect this one is, then you need my help even more than I first thought."

Leigh leaned on the counter behind her, but the few inches of distance she gained did nothing to ease the tension mounting within her. Her senses were reeling, and she knew her turmoil had less to do with Mitch's threatening glower than with the simple fact that he was standing close enough for her to discern mesmerizing flecks of emerald in the dark silver of his eyes. She'd been feeling odd sensations rushing through her ever since his big hands had clamped onto her shoulders, and she realized now that they weren't tremors of fear but tingles of excitement. Lord, what was happening to her?

"So are you?" he demanded.

Leigh didn't even pretend not to understand what he was asking, and some unstudied impulse made her shake her head. "No. I'm not sleeping with Vinnie."

She could have sworn it was relief that showed in the sudden relaxing of his tall, sinewy frame, but the glint in his eyes was one of purely masculine satisfaction, and Leigh was afraid to ponder what that might mean.

"Good," he pronounced, his tone a verbal pat on the head. "Now you can eat your toast."

"Thanks, but I've suddenly lost my appetite."

Dropping his hands to his sides, Mitch glanced around her at the flattened toast. "I can't say I blame you. Maybe I'll take you to lunch while we're out."

Leigh's eyes widened. "Out where?"

"Don't look so scared," he chuckled. "You're safe now that I'm with you."

"I'm not scared," she lied, "just cautious. Except for the grocery store, I've been sticking pretty close to home."

"That was smart while you were staying alone. But if we're going to spend a few more days here, I need some things that I doubt the local grocery store will have. I noticed exit signs for a shopping mall on the way up. We'll go there."

"What kind of things?" Leigh pressed. "Maybe you could borrow what you need from my brother-in-law."

"What size is he?"

She examined the width of Mitch's shoulders and the long, lean line from his waist to the floor, and her hopeful expression faded. "Not the same size as you, I'm sure."

"It's probably just as well," he told her. "I can use some shirts and stuff anyway. I hate to shop, so I don't bother unless I'm forced into it."

"Like now?" Leigh sighed.

"Like now. So go get your jacket."

"I don't suppose you'd consider the possibility of going alone?"

"Not for a second."

"Is this the way this protective custody business is always handled?" she groused. "By hounding the person night and day?"

"I don't know," he countered easily. "Or care. This is the way *I* intend to do it."

She took a reluctant step toward the doorway, tossing back over her shoulder, "Then why didn't you come better prepared?"

"Believe me, I thought I was."

Something in his soft tone beckoned her attention, and she turned to find him staring after her with a strangely bemused expression.

"Well," she said awkwardly, "it strikes me as pretty poor advance planning. I'm not so sure I feel any safer going out with you than I did alone."

With two long strides Mitch was by her side. Almost absently he lifted his hand and brushed from her cheek a wispy curl that had escaped the thick coil of hair anchored at the nape of her neck. Even that light touch unfurled streamers of new sensations that both confused and beguiled her.

"I like your hair better the way you had it last night," he said quietly. "All soft and loose."

"Thanks for telling me; I'll make a point of wearing it pulled back while you're here."

He cocked a brow sardonically, obviously more amused

by her irritability than he'd been by her joking earlier. "Don't fret, angel, I'm not going to let anybody hurt you—not even myself. Now run and get your jacket."

She did as he ordered, grateful to escape even for a moment the intensity of his dark gaze and the staggering challenge his nearness presented to her senses. All those fine, gallant claims he'd made to protect her from harm sure sounded good. But who, she worried as she donned the slightly battle-rumpled rose parka, was going to protect her from herself?

By the time they arrived at the mall in nearby York, Mitch had decided he was too hungry to wait for lunch, so their first stop was for brunch at a small coffee shop. Afterward, watching him glance down the long row of stores and specialty shops in utter confusion, Leigh took pity on him and asked exactly what he needed to buy. Gratefully, he rattled off a short list of items, which she decided could all be found in the men's department of a large store at the opposite end of the mall.

On their way there they passed a toy shop, and on impulse Leigh decided to pick up a couple of toys to leave behind as a surprise for her niece and nephew when they returned home. She quickly selected a large bespectacled leopard she knew would satisfy Kristen's passion for stuffed animals, then turned in an effort to include Mitch in the fun.

"Okay, it's your turn. What do you think would please a seven-year-old boy?" She added affectionately, "A very active seven-year-old."

"A robot bank with a detachable head," he countered promptly, his expression one of stark disgust.

Leigh smiled. "Cute, but something tells me he already has one."

"Had one. After I finished picking up the pennies—several hundred of them—I couldn't get the damn head back on. It's not funny," he added as she struggled to subdue a grin.

"Of course not to you," Leigh managed between giggles. "You have no sense of humor, remember?"

"It's not that I don't have *any* sense of humor," he protested. "I just don't go around joking and laughing like an idiot all the time—especially over things that aren't the least bit funny."

Leigh's grin broadened. "Fine, but I think you should know that this idiot thinks the idea of you scurrying around picking up pennies and stuffing them into a headless robot is extremely funny...comical...uproarious..."

"I get the idea," he interrupted, jerking on her hand to move her away from the curious stares of the gum-chewing clerks stocking shelves nearby. "Now can we just find another stupid bank and get out of here?"

They found a passable replacement for the broken bank, and with Mitch's stoic assistance Leigh decided on something called an Interstellar Transport Vehicle for Michael's gift. She was so intrigued by the fact that it had flashing lights and made six different space-age noises that she didn't notice the small print at the bottom of the box until it was paid for and being slipped into a bag.

"Oh no!" she cried, drawing identical strange looks from the clerk and Mitch. "It says: 'Assembly Required.'"

"So?" Mitch inquired.

"So I never would have picked it if I'd known that."

He shifted impatiently. "Leigh, it's just a toy. How difficult can it be to put together?"

"Very. Last Christmas it took me six hours to assemble a small man-eating alligator, and then I finally had to break two pieces to get them to fit." Her lips formed a regretful frown. "I never did get it to actually eat the little men either."

Mitch gave her another of those funny looks—somewhere between disbelief and enchantment—and nodded at the waiting clerk to finish bagging the toy. "I'll put it together for you," he said to Leigh.

"Oh, I couldn't let you do tha——"

She abruptly broke off the instinctively polite protest as fleeting images of her experiences with this man pranced through her head. She'd known him less than twenty-four hours, and so far he had embarrassed, harassed, bullied, wrestled, and kissed her into submission. The sight of him struggling with hundreds of tiny pieces of plastic and ten pages of complicated instructions would be eminently soul satisfying.

Flashing him a brilliantly demure smile, she said, "Thank you, Mitch, that would be wonderful."

Mitch stared at her. That docilely feminine flutter of long eyelashes didn't fool him for one second. He could see past them to the mischief sparkling in her deep blue eyes. The woman was an enigma—part tiger, part lamb—and always tilting him off-balance. And, he realized in amazement, he was loving every minute of it.

Well, not *every* minute. Those first few after he'd left her bedroom last night had been pure hell as he fought an impulse he'd never had to struggle to tame before: the urge to take her. Usually when he wanted a woman the feeling was reciprocated. If not, he simply put the feeling and the woman out of his mind.

But no matter how hard he tried, he hadn't been able to banish the memory of Leigh lying in his arms. It had haunted him all night, adding to the restlessness he'd learned to live with, and it was with him now as they walked side by side, weaving a path through the early-morning shoppers. Just that brief encounter had managed to sear the taste and feel and scent of her into his consciousness to the point where they seemed as familiar and as much a part of him as his own name.

It was while lying there awake, the feeling of her still burning his flesh, that he'd decided he had to make her want him as much as he wanted her. This little shopping expedition had seemed like a good way to start. It was the kind of outing he supposed a woman would like, a way to get her to relax with him. Although after struggling through a nearly silent brunch and that trip through the toy store, Mitch was beginning to wonder if he shouldn't have just kept her at home and tried to charm her in a less subtle way.

Once they were inside the department store, he let Leigh take the lead, trailing along behind as she zoomed in on the men's department like a homing pigeon.

Stopping by one of the neatly arranged display tables, she announced with an efficient sweep of her arm, "Shirts. How many do you think you'll need?"

"Three," he decided arbitrarily.

How should he know how many shirts he would need when he still didn't know how long he would be here? Not that he had any intention of pressuring her on that point. He was in no hurry to return and confront DeMarco until he knew all the facts. He was in even less of a hurry to end his self-appointed role as her live-in protector.

Quickly scanning the row of shirts nearest him, he located three in his size and tucked them under his arm. "All set. What's next?"

Leigh's surprised gaze traveled from his face to the shirts and back. "What do you mean all set? Those are all the same color."

"Right."

"But they're all black."

He shrugged. "I like black. It matches my jeans. Most of them are black, too."

"That's the stupidest thing I ever heard."

Mitch directed his scowl at the display of shirts. He didn't mind being called stupid—especially about something as unimportant as what color shirts he wore—but he didn't like being on the receiving end of that overtly disapproving look Leigh was flashing. Maybe the color shirts a man wore *was* important to her. It had been longer than a long time since he'd cared enough about a woman to dress to please her; it had been forever. And he had no idea why he felt inclined to do it now. Or how to go about it.

"What color do you think I should get?" he asked finally.

"I suppose black is the right choice after all for a man in your line of work—what with all that skulking around in the shadows you probably have to do."

"I don't skulk," he denied hotly, wondering if sitting in his Jeep watching her yesterday qualified as skulking.

Leigh rolled her eyes. "I was only teasing."

Teasing. She did a lot of that, and he always managed to respond in the wrong way, Mitch realized ruefully.

"All right," he ventured a little more roughly than he intended, "what would you recommend for days when I'm not skulking?"

She shrugged. "I really couldn't care less."

Her cool indifference irked him even more than her disapproval had. Glaring at the neat, color-coordinated rows of tailored shirts, he tried to remember which ones she'd been examining when he'd announced he was all set. The blue and white pinstripe he could handle, he decided, but the pale pink one she'd fingered briefly was definitely out. Unless it turned out to be her favorite.

Hoping that wasn't the case, or that she at least wouldn't torture him by saying so, he tossed back one of the black shirts and picked up the striped one. Then, with reckless abandon, he added a solid yellow one to the pile under his arm before turning to face her. The approval he sought was there all right, mixed with a hint of indulgent amusement he wasn't accustomed to receiving from women. But then, he wasn't accustomed to women like Leigh.

Cautiously, he allowed himself to be led to the sock and underwear section. With one eye on her reaction, he chose a half-dozen pair of the same black wool socks he always wore, then held his breath as he turned to the underwear. He'd never worn anything other than basic white, and he wasn't going to start now . . . even if it did sound as if she muttered a soft, laugh-tinged "Boring" under her breath as he reached for a package of briefs.

He added a new pair of jeans without bothering to try them on, then paid for all of it and hoisted the bulky bag in the arm not weighed down with toys.

"Need a hand?" Leigh asked, eyeing his struggle.

"No," he grunted, "I can manage."

"Fine."

Despite her little smile, Mitch had a feeling the trip wasn't turning out as well as he'd hoped. He'd wanted them to get to know each other better so Leigh would realize that she could trust him. Until she felt close enough to him to tell him the truth about her problems, he couldn't solve them for her. And until he did, he had to keep up this damn pretense of being a federal agent.

He hated lying to her, but he knew if he told her now who he really was—a bounty hunter hired by De-

Marco—she wouldn't give him half a chance to explain the rest. She'd no doubt try to run again, and he couldn't allow that. That would only put her in more danger. And if he had to resort to tying her up to keep her with him, she'd probably feel even less inclined to talk than she did now.

Shifting his awkward hold on the bags, he glanced to his side and suddenly realized he was walking alone. Instantly his heart slammed into his ribs, and all the air was expelled from his lungs in one wild rasp. She'd tricked him! his brain screamed, fear and anger rising in tandem. But even as he turned, berating himself for not watching her more closely, he caught a glimpse of the rose parka through a small herd of old ladies tottering past, and he began to breathe again.

Stalking back to where she stood peering at a sidewalk display outside a gift shop, he snapped, "What the hell do you think you're doing?"

She flicked him with a brief, disparaging glance. "Browsing. That's not unusual when one is at a shopping mall."

Mitch pondered that. He couldn't very well blast her for doing exactly what he'd brought her here for. "Well, you should have told me you were going to stop," he declared finally.

"Why? Do you get demerits for losing a prisoner?"

"You're not a prisoner..." He shifted uncomfortably as she leveled him with an uncompromisingly pointed stare, then added, "...exactly."

"Well, a prisoner is *exactly* what I feel like. And if I'm not going to be allowed to take a step without you, why don't you just handcuff me to your side?"

Calmer now, Mitch decided it was better to let the

whole subject drop. He glanced down at the table where an array of heart-shaped boxes of candy surrounded a sign reminding passing lovers that Valentine's Day was only a week away. Maybe he should buy her one, he thought ... as a sort of peace offering. She might be touched and decide he wasn't such an ogre after all. On the other hand, she might laugh right in his face.

"Do you like these?" he asked in an attempt to sound casual.

Leigh shrugged, but when she looked up at him there was a sheepish half-smile forming where the icy, mocking one had been a moment ago.

"I used to," she admitted. "I was twelve the year my sister Debby became engaged. Mike gave her a box of candy just like this for Valentine's Day." She pointed out a large satin-covered box topped with a bride doll in full lacy regalia. "I was green with envy. I used to lie in bed at night and dream of the day when some man would come along and give me one, too."

Mitch smiled at the whimsical tone she'd taken on as she spoke.

"I can see how that would catch a kid's eye," he agreed. "But I think I'd rather hear about what kind of man you used to dream of."

He watched as a flustered shade of pink instantly invaded Leigh's cheeks.

"Not your kind!" she retorted sharply.

Mitch gritted his teeth. What in hell had he said wrong this time? Grabbing the box of candy off the table, he strode inside to pay for it, then thrust it into the hands of a startled-looking Leigh.

"Here," he growled. "Just in case your dream man

never shows up." Mashing both bags under one arm so he could keep a firm grip on her elbow with the other, he began dragging her toward the nearest exit. "And I'll think about the handcuffs."

Chapter Four

EXCEPT FOR THE dinner of shrimp feta that Leigh spent all afternoon in the kitchen preparing, the rest of the day was a dismal failure. He couldn't seem to move her one inch closer to trusting him—or liking him—and Mitch wasn't sure which bothered him the most.

He needed her to trust him in order to put this whole thing behind them, but he wanted even more for her to like him. If he couldn't accomplish that, it would all be over as soon as she was safe from DeMarco. The problem was, he hadn't any idea how to go about making her like him. Mitch cursed softly. That was the heart of the problem right there: He couldn't *make* her like him. Damn, it was so much easier just to pick up a woman in a bar. Then she knew what your angle was right up front and could decide whether to accept or decline while she sipped the drink you bought her.

This thing with Leigh was something much more complicated, and even he wasn't sure exactly what his angle was yet. He only knew he wanted her and that he didn't want to rush things and take her under false pretenses or by storming her defenses the way he had the other night. He wanted her warm and willing. But except for buying her a drink and scorching her with lustful looks, he wasn't sure how to make a woman feel that way. Not a woman like Leigh anyway. A woman whose life had focus and balance and a purpose that went deeper than the next brief affair. A woman who could manage to do something as simple as breathe or walk across a room with such a tantalizing blend of innocence and sensuality that for the first time in years he found he was hungry to get close to a woman *outside* of bed.

It wasn't that he'd gone out of his way to avoid women like her in the past. He just seldom came into contact with any. And if he did, Mitch acknowledged realistically, they would probably do all the avoiding necessary. It had been a long time since he'd been any woman's idea of a man she'd like to bring home to mother—if indeed he ever had been. He sure wasn't the right man for Leigh. He'd known even without being told that a bounty hunter without any real roots wasn't the sort of man she dreamed about. But that hardly mattered under the circumstances. She was vulnerable and in trouble and in need of protection—a man's protection. His protection. Hell, there was no one else.

He was sure of one other thing, too. Leigh wasn't going to come around by herself. Which meant he was going to have to start off another day by apologizing to her. And that wasn't one of his finer talents either.

"Good morning, Leigh," he said when she walked

into the kitchen a little after seven the next morning. "Can I pour you a cup of coffee?"

Her hand already on the pot handle, she turned to flick him a sardonic look. "Thanks. I can manage."

Shaking his head at his own ineptitude, Mitch ambled across the kitchen to lean against the counter a few feet away from her. Dressed in jeans and a fuzzy white sweater, she was more beautiful than the sunrise he'd just watched. Everything she wore looked soft and pale, the way she'd been that night in his arms. Mitch ached to touch her.

Instead, he cleared his throat and began hesitantly, "Listen, Leigh, about yesterday . . . I know I wasn't very much help in the toy store and I'm, uh, sorry I yelled at you." He shrugged. "I only wanted you to relax and enjoy yourself."

"You've got to be kidding!" she countered, whirling to gape at him in disbelief.

He shook his head. "No. I mean it. I knew you'd been stuck in here alone for days and that you weren't too thrilled to have me for company. I thought going to the mall would be . . . fun."

"Fun?" she wailed. "You think it's fun having granite-man for a Siamese twin?"

Mitch winced. "I don't think I'm that bad."

"You're worse. You can't take a joke. You're suspicious of everything and everybody. You're constantly trying to pry information out of me. You stalk me wherever I go—"

"I didn't stalk you," he interjected.

"You followed me to the ladies' room in the restaurant, for heaven's sake."

"Not inside."

"Only because there was another woman in there."

Slamming her cup down on the counter, she seethed, "Believe me, yesterday will not live in my memory as a day of fun and frolic."

"I know. That's why I'm apologizing," he countered quietly. "Today will be better."

"Why? Are you leaving?"

He sighed. "No. But I thought we could do something you'd enjoy." All of a sudden the great idea he'd come up with while she slept seemed a lot less brilliant. "I noticed you playing in the snow the other day, just before I rang the bell, and I thought maybe you'd like to make a snowman together later . . . or something," he added a little lamely.

Leigh listened to the proposal in silence. When he finished she shook her head in complete bafflement.

"Cutter, what is it with you anyway? Ever since you forced your way into my life you've been making me feel like some sort of criminal, and—"

"I haven't meant to," he broke in, his gruff, earnest tone swaying her slightly from the cool disdain she was determined to feel toward him.

"Then you'll be pleased to learn you have the natural talent to go along with your badge," she retorted, noting that the flush it brought to his cheeks did not seem to be one of pride. "Yesterday you were threatening me with handcuffs, and this morning you're coming on like the activities director for a cruise ship. Do you want to be my bodyguard, Cutter, or my friend?"

"Both," he replied firmly. "Leigh, until you come clean with me, I don't know for sure how much danger you're really in. And I don't think you do either. But I do know that DeMarco can play rough. You *need* me to look out for you right now, and I think maybe I . . . could use a friend."

Leigh had to bite back a smile at the meticulous way he avoided using the word *need* in relation to himself. His voice was grim, controlled, but she detected a pleading hesitancy in his silvery gaze. It was almost a yearning look, but a very different one from that which had blazed in his eyes that night in her bed. This look had little to do with sex and everything to do with need, and it melted the wall of resistance she had spent the past twenty-four hours constructing into a puddle of compassion.

Taking a lazy sip of her coffee, she ran her gaze critically from his dark shirt to the toes of his leather boots.

"You look—and sound—as if you belong on a ranch somewhere," she scoffed. "I'll bet you don't even know how to make a snowman."

Mitch's lips twisted into a slow smile. "We didn't get a whole lot of snow where I grew up in Texas," he admitted. "But I'm a real fast learner."

"Good. Because I'm a very demanding teacher."

"Promise?" he drawled as she headed back to her room, the single, soft word trailing after her like a challenge.

In the end—at Mitch's insistence—they set out to make a snow fort instead of a snowman. Then Leigh discovered a slightly battered funnel behind the woodpile, the perfect mold for turning his square, unimaginative lookout towers into graceful spires.

"Have you always had this obsession with castles?" he asked, standing back to watch her put the finishing touch on the project they'd been working on for most of the afternoon. "First you buy a castle to turn it into an inn, and now you're turning my fort into a castle."

It did look like a castle, an enchanted one, Leigh decided, noting the way the snow crystals shimmered like diamonds in the late afternoon sun. Or maybe it was simply that the whole afternoon was enchanted. For sure, something magical and mysterious had happened as they worked side by side, turning the carefully formed blocks of snow into a domed structure that stood as high as her shoulders. She was actually starting to think of Mitch as a friend instead of a bodyguard. So much so that she was able to laugh at his remark about castles, when only hours ago it would have made her wary and defensive.

"I guess I do have a thing for castles," she admitted unabashedly. "In fact, I used to dream about being a princess. Of course, that was before I progressed to dreaming about bride dolls and valentines," she added, a self-deprecating cast to her smile.

"A fairy-tale princess?" Mitch inquired, his own smile easy and warm. "Like the one who could detect a pea even through a mountain of mattresses?"

"I never got that specific in my dreams. But I was definitely going to have a castle—and a prince—and live happily ever after." Her smile dissolved into a frown that rippled her forehead. "All I ended up with was the castle . . . maybe."

Mitch moved closer, until she could feel the leather sleeve of his jacket rasping against the nylon of hers. "Is it because of the castle that you're in trouble, Leigh? Is that why you went to DeMarco for money?"

Leigh swallowed hard, the urge to tell him—to tell someone—suddenly a palpable force inside her. Never before had she wrestled alone with such a mammoth problem. But then never before, she thought disgustedly, had she been stupid enough to crawl out on such a flimsy limb.

"I'm not in trouble," she insisted weakly. "I'm simply paying the consequences for taking some foolish chances."

She winced at her own poor choice of words. She would pay gladly if only she had a cent to her name to pay with.

"What sort of chances?"

"Buying the inn in the first place," she responded without taking time to measure her words. "Thinking that my training and experience managing hotels for others qualified me to undertake something like this on my own."

"How much training and experience do you have?" Mitch asked. His tone was relaxed, interested rather than interrogating, and Leigh found herself responding.

"Six years' worth, ever since I graduated from college. I started out managing my folks' restaurant in Narragansett. When they decided to retire and move to Florida, they wanted me to take it over completely, but I refused."

"Why?"

"Because I *used* to be smart," she countered dryly. "I hate taking risks; it's just not in my nature. Instead, I went to work managing a large restaurant in Newport; then I was offered the manager's position at one of the smaller hotels along the wharf there. I did a good job, too . . . until I got this bright idea."

He smiled at her disgusted shudder. "To go into business for yourself?"

"Right. I'm sure it would have passed—like any incidence of temporary insanity—but I made the mistake of mentioning it to my sister and a friend of mine—"

"Vinnie?" he interrupted, turning the name into a formidable snarl.

Leigh leaned forward to pat the already perfect surface of a castle arch, keeping her burgeoning grin carefully concealed behind a curtain of dark hair. "As a matter of fact, no. This friend's name happens to be Mark. He's the head chef at a hotel in Newport now, but we've been friends since we worked together during college."

"I see."

His terse tone told Leigh that he did not find whatever he saw—or thought he saw—pleasing, and for some reason that pleased her very much.

"Anyway," she went on, cheerfully ignoring his scowl, "together Debby and Mark managed to convince me that I should go for it, that buying the inn was a once-in-a-lifetime opportunity."

"So you did it."

She nodded.

"Except you didn't have quite enough money to cinch the deal, and Eddie DeMarco was only too willing to front you what you needed."

Leigh shifted her gaze away from his. She suddenly felt trapped and decidedly less cheerful than she had a moment ago. Buying the inn had been her first mistake. Mitch had just come close to hitting on her second. She couldn't afford to make a third by trusting a man she knew even less than she had known Vinnie, even if his gray eyes did seem to promise all the understanding and support she longed for.

"I told you," she said, staring down at the shiny toes of her white rubber boots. "I never went to see DeMarco. For money or for any other reason."

"And I believe you. I also believe that your pal Vinnie did the asking for you and that you didn't have any idea of what you were getting into when you let him do it." He sighed. "Look at me, Leigh."

She did and found his expression grave, his eyes filled with tender concern in a way that warmed her in spite of her uneasiness.

"I'm not going to press you to tell me now, angel," he promised softly. "But I want you to know that when you do tell me, you can trust me to handle it for you, to do what's best for you and you alone."

Leigh stared at him in confusion. "But your job . . . what about . . . ?"

"My job doesn't matter," he declared. "The only one who matters to me in this whole thing is you." He reached out and cupped her chin in his leather-clad palm. "Don't you know that you've become less of a job and more of a woman to me with every moment I've been here?"

Leigh drew a deep breath and watched it billow back out in a misty puff. She was flattered . . . and terrified. "I don't understand . . ."

"Neither do I," he admitted with a wry smile when she trailed off. "Believe me, what I'm feeling is the last thing I expected to feel when I headed up here to find you. I figured you'd be some dizzy broad who—" He broke off with an uneasy shrug. "What I expected you to be doesn't matter anymore."

He was holding her face with both gloved hands now, and Leigh felt her senses begin to flutter in response to the light touch and in anticipation of what she knew was about to happen if she didn't move away in a hurry. She stayed, excitement mounting within her in a steadily tightening coil as she watched Mitch's eyes grow dark and hungry.

"This prince you mentioned," he said softly, "how did you used to find him in your dreams?"

"Usually he found me," she replied, her eyes widening as she realized how prophetic that sounded. "I mean, he was just always there . . . he sort of came with the castle."

"A package deal?"

"Something like that."

"I see. Then you never had to kiss a frog to turn him into a prince?"

Leigh hesitated. There was laughter lurking in his dark eyes, and she realized in slow amazement that he was attempting to be playful, to joke with her. She released a smile, and with it came the flood of tenderness she'd been struggling to control.

"No, there were never any frogs in my dreams at all." She lifted her hands, touching his snow-speckled black beard with her mittens. In a movement that was instinctive and shattering in its vulnerability, he nestled his cheek against the soft white wool that sheathed her hand. And in that instant Leigh's fate was sealed.

In a whisper tinged with laughter, she said, "Oh, Mitch, you're far from being a frog."

"And even further from being a prince," he countered with a gruff laugh. "But do you think we could give it a try anyway?"

He didn't wait for her answer. His dark head bent to hers with implacable intent. Leigh felt first his frost-tinged beard brushing against her chin; then her senses received a wild surge of pleasure and alarm as his mouth opened over hers, searing her with heat that was damp and erotic. Instinctively, she gave way to the demanding thrust of his tongue and felt it sweep inside to caress the smooth, sensitive walls of her mouth, creating in her a whole new sonata of sensations and longings that she felt all the way to her core.

There was none of the roughness of their first kiss, yet this one was every bit as aggressive. Mitch kissed, she realized hazily, the way he did everything else—with crushing determination and total control. She found she enjoyed being kissed that way, in spite of the newly discovered, irksome streak of independence that suggested she shouldn't. Ignoring it, she rested her hands on his shoulders and surrendered to the waves of pleasure washing over them.

As the light wind sent snowflakes dancing around them, his kiss grew more urgent. His hands, which had dropped from her face to her hips, became more insistent, urging her steadily closer until his arousal was pressed firmly against her belly. Leigh promised herself she would heed the unmistakable warning as soon as the pounding sweetness inside subsided.

She was vaguely aware of his hand moving along her hip, sliding beneath the knitted waistband of her jacket and the hem of her sweater, but only when the chill air touched her bare skin did the reality of his boldness pierce the sensual web he'd woven. And then it was too late. His hand was a rough, heated blanket settling firmly, possessively around her breast, and Leigh was suddenly far too warm to feel cold.

His fingers moved on the full upper slope in a light, circular caress, while his thumb grazed her nipple, gliding back and forth with lazy strokes that filled her with excitement. Leigh felt the instinctive firming of her nipple in response to his touch and at the same time felt a much more subtle flowering taking place within. She knew what she was feeling was much more complicated, and no doubt more dangerous, than plain old lust. Mitch Cutter was beginning to stir up feelings she'd thought were quite well barricaded behind the cautious habits of a lifetime.

Ever since the night he'd carried her back to her bed, she'd been telling herself that the power he'd seemed to exert over her senses had been a figment of an imagination driven into overdrive by sheer fright. She knew now that that power was very real and even more potent than she'd first feared. He was creating in her a desire that was all new and white-hot in intensity, pushing her toward some new frontier of sensation with a studied ease she should probably resent but didn't.

She was too caught up in the pleasure pulsing through her, too eager to see where it would lead, to resent the claim he was staking. Or to protest. Or to realize that she was standing in the middle of her sister's backyard, in broad daylight, yielding to the intimate caresses of a man who, up until a few hours ago, she'd been trying to convince herself she hated.

Reluctantly, Mitch lifted his mouth from hers. "Oh, sweet woman, you are so soft," he whispered hoarsely. "A man could get lost in something as soft and sweet as you are."

His hand on her breast continued to move gently, but something dangerous and unfathomable swirled in the hot-silver depths of his eyes, as if he wasn't sure whether or not he liked the idea of being that man. Leigh felt a flicker of regret. At that moment, she was very sure of what she wanted. She just wasn't sure she wanted to risk reaching out for it. On some unexplainable level of understanding, she knew that offering love to Mitch and asking for it in return would be a bigger risk, and a potentially more devastating one, than tangling with Eddie De-Marco. A shudder ran through her at how close she was to taking that risk.

"Damn, you're so cold, you're shivering," Mitch muttered instantly. "And I'm a fool for keeping you out here like this when we have a nice warm house waiting for us."

With a sigh of regret, he slid his hand from beneath her jacket and tugged the fabric snugly over her hips.

As soon as his hands fell away, Leigh replaced them with her own, proceeding to tug at the waistband with motions that were revealingly skittish.

"It is cold out here," she agreed. "And I should go in and start dinner. You must be starving after all this work out in the cold air. I know I am. I thought I'd make an eggplant casserole tonight. That is, if you like eggplant. Of course my mother always says that anything tastes good if you're hungry enough."

She had started trudging across the yard as she spoke, aware that she was rambling nervously, and even more aware of the man walking close beside her. As they reached the side door, he stretched one long arm in front of her to grasp the knob, effectively halting her retreat and forcing her to confront the silent amusement in his eyes.

"You are hungry, aren't you?" she asked for want of something more intelligent to say.

"Starving." The word was a soft, husky caress, unmistakable in meaning.

"Good," she responded with intentional obliqueness. "I'll get started right away."

"Can I help?" he asked, following her upstairs after they'd shed their wet boots and coats in the garage.

The idea of being trapped in the kitchen with him, trying to follow the intricacies of a new recipe under his watchful gaze, sent Leigh into a panic. She needed time alone to sort out the chaotic tangle of her emotions. Searching frantically for an excuse to get rid of him, her eyes fell on the Interstellar Transport Vehicle still in its box on the hall table.

Grabbing it with both hands, she turned and thrust it into the arms of a startled Mitch, almost tumbling him back down the stairs in her enthusiastic relief.

"Here!" she exclaimed. "You can help by putting this together." When he looked as if he was about to refuse, she added, "You did promise."

"So I did."

"And now you're having second thoughts."

"Not about putting it together for you. It just wasn't how I envisioned spending this evening."

How he *had* envisioned spending it was obvious enough to bring a flush to Leigh's cheeks. "Look, if you don't think you can handle it, just say so."

His brows lowered to a fierce angle. "Woman, you're talking to a man who built a scale model of a P-40 Curtis War Hawk when he was twelve."

"No kidding?" Leigh let her expression of wide-eyed awe dwindle. "What's a P-40 Curtis War Hawk?"

Mitch sighed disgustedly. "A plane used during World War II. I built the whole series: the P-38 Lockheed Lightning, the P-39 Belle Air Cobra—I even had one of the original A-20 Havocs."

Leigh gave a long, low whistle. "You don't say. A genuine A-20 Havoc, huh? That sure must have been something. I don't think I've ever heard you speak of anything so affectionately." Her eyes sparkled like dark sapphires. "Why, I'll bet those planes still have a place of honor in your bedroom, too. Your own version of the classic etchings lure."

"Not quite." Beneath the dark mustache Mitch's mouth drew into a hard line that was distinctively humorless. "We moved from Fort Bliss in Texas to Fort Ord when I was fourteen, and my father decided the planes were too awkward to pack. He also decided I was too old to be playing with them. I left them behind with a kid I knew."

"Your father was in the army?" Leigh asked, partly

to change the subject from one that obviously bothered him, and partly to delve into the first hint he'd ever given about who he was or where he came from.

"That's right, a general." There was an unmistakable edge to the clipped reply.

"My brother-in-law is a commander in the navy," she offered. "As a matter of fact, that's why he and my sister are in Scotland now, so he can review a shipyard there. So I know the military can be a hard life in some ways. I'm sure it was tough for you growing up—moving all the time and all. And for your mother, too."

He shrugged, but there was a flicker of pain in his eyes, and he focused on a point somewhere over her shoulder. "My mother died when I was five. After that there was just Dad and I, literally, for the most part. It's tough enough making friends when you're always the new kid on the block. It's even worse when your father is the boss of all the other kids' fathers on the base."

"I guess it helped to have a hobby—the models, that is."

"It helped," he agreed, but there was none of the earlier pleasure in his tone. "It also helped for him to make me leave them behind, although I hated him for it at the time. It taught me the most important lesson I've ever learned: that you should never have anything that it would really hurt you to lose." His mouth twisted into a cold parody of a smile as he added, "My own secret for finding complete happiness."

It sounded like complete insanity to Leigh. And so achingly sad that all semblance of a casual response dried on her tongue. Finally, as he stood there shifting the toy box in his hands, watching her in increasingly awkward silence, she forced a half-smile.

"Well, I guess we all have our own ideas of happiness.

I think mine is being saddled with a bodyguard who also happens to have experience assembling model airplanes. I just hope you don't find this space-age variety too much of a challenge."

As she turned to make her escape into the kitchen, she caught the wry smile that softened the corners of his lips, and she didn't dare turn back as his soft reply drifted after her.

"At least *this* challenge is one I think I can handle."

He left the rest of the thought unspoken, and Leigh spent the hour and a half it took her to prepare dinner mulling over exactly which challenge he thought he *couldn't* handle. He couldn't possibly consider *her* a challenge. Lord, she'd practically melted in his arms both times he'd kissed her, and both times she had *not* been the one to put an end to it. No, she definitely was not presenting him with much of a challenge in that department, she admitted uneasily.

She couldn't think of any other way she could possibly challenge him. He'd proved he was the superior wrestler, and she had obviously acquiesced to his role as her bodyguard. Then it hit her like a bolt of lightning, and Leigh froze with the hot casserole halfway out of the oven. Information. That was what she had that he wanted. Information and her cooperation with the investigation he was part of.

How could she have let herself forget even for a moment why he was here? That he was not a friend but a man who was being paid to watch her and to chip away at her resistance. And that talk about her being a woman to him now instead of merely a job . . . that's all it was, talk. Most likely a carefully rehearsed line he'd had success with in the past. And the kiss. That was probably in the line of duty as well.

Even as the bitter thought filtered through her brain, some part of Leigh rejected it. There had been something in the kiss—and in his expression afterward—that had been genuine. She didn't know how she knew that, but she did. And that certainty was enough to let her heart override her common sense and keep the embers of whatever emotion she'd begun to feel toward him burning inside. It was also enough to keep her from feeling utterly used and humiliated and storming out to the living room to tell him she'd had it with this whole scenario.

It was not enough, however, to keep her from gathering her defenses around her with fresh determination as she carried the tray holding the casserole and plates out to the coffee table where he was working.

When she noticed that he was idly thumbing through an old magazine instead of delivering impassioned oaths to a sea of tiny plastic pieces, she asked smugly, "Give up already?"

"No," he replied, tossing the magazine down and nodding at the mantel behind her. "I finished nearly an hour ago."

Leigh swung around to find the toy sitting there, fully assembled right down to the last sleek wing and flashing taillight. Hurriedly placing the tray on the coffee table, she crossed to the fireplace and systematically tested all the switches and buttons, growing more and more disgusted as she discovered they all worked just as the box had suggested they should.

"You really did it," she said finally.

"You sound disappointed."

"I *was* looking forward to seeing you pull your hair out," she admitted. "Especially that beard."

Mitch touched his chin consideringly. "You don't like my beard?"

"I don't like beards, period. It's nothing personal."

"Does it bother you when I kiss you?" he persisted.

Leigh hesitated. She'd really backed herself into a corner with this one. She could hardly admit that she was beginning to like the feel of it against her skin, that it aroused her and gave full rein to all sorts of tactile imaginings. Or that it probably had a lot to do with his rugged, masculine appeal and the corresponding fact that she'd been tossing and turning long into the night.

"It doesn't bother me especially," she said finally, shrugging with a casualness she was far from feeling. "Why? Would you even resort to shaving your beard to get the job done?"

His eyes narrowed in wary confusion. "What's that supposed to mean?"

"You know, your job," she countered airily. "Getting the witness to crack and all that. Only I must admit, you're using a more subtle approach than the glaring lights and colorful threats I've seen in movies."

"And just what approach is that?" he asked softly, too softly.

"You know, this whole thing." Under his stormy regard, her hand fluttered spastically, and the note of cool control began to drain from her voice. "The kiss, the snow castle . . . all of it."

"Is that what you think I was doing? Trying to soften you up so you'd cooperate?"

"Weren't you?" The question was a quivering whisper, laden with a hopefulness she hated but couldn't disguise.

"No," he growled, "and I think maybe it's time I proved that to you once and for all."

Chapter Five

MITCH WAS OFF the sofa and beating a menacing path around the Queen Anne chair that stood between them before the full magnitude of what he planned hit him. He'd issued the threat unthinkingly, in anger, but it was something that had been building inside him for hours. No, for days. He was going to prove to Leigh Bramwell that she was more than a damned assignment to him in the most elemental way a man could prove such a thing to a woman.

And judging from the look of skittish horror on her face, she understood precisely what he had in mind. Good. He'd wasted enough time tiptoeing around her, trying to do things the honorable way. She was no closer to trusting him or confiding in him now than she was when he'd first pushed his way in here. His father and all his commanding officers in the army and his superiors on the police force had been right about one thing: He just couldn't do things in an orthodox manner. He had his own style, his own way of getting results, and the sooner Leigh came to terms with that, the better.

He might not know how to woo her trust, but he damn well knew how to make her his. And he knew from her response to him outside that deep down that was what Leigh wanted, too, if she'd only let down her guard long enough to admit it. Once he staked his claim on her he would have a right to protect her, a right to ask questions and demand the truth instead of these evasive, half-answers she'd been tossing at him whenever he got too close. Leigh would understand that kind of commitment. And she would also understand that he'd stretched the truth in the first place solely for her own good. Then they could stop this damned charade and he could make her see that his reason for protecting her had nothing to do with his job and everything to do with these unfamiliar feelings inside that he couldn't even tag a name on yet.

At least he *hoped* she would understand. Watching her as she backed warily away from him, Mitch knew an instant of heavy doubt. The woman didn't always react to a crisis in the most logical, levelheaded manner. Abruptly, he dismissed the thought. He couldn't worry about that now. He'd decided while he sat there snapping together hundreds of small plastic aircraft parts that his plan to charm Leigh into trusting him wasn't going to work, and a more direct approach was called for. Time was running out and he wanted to—needed to—bind her to him in the only way he knew how.

As if reading the fresh determination in him, Leigh abruptly stopped her hedging movements and whirled to flee through the narrow passage between the sofa and coffee table. With one quick sidestep, Mitch cut her off. He was about to reach for her when she grappled for the bottle of wine on the dinner tray and held it aloft in what he supposed was intended to be a threatening manner.

"Hold it," she ordered. "Or so help me I'll . . . I'll . . ."

"Drown me?" he offered helpfully, amusement mingling briefly with the impatience and tension within. "For godsake, Leigh, put the bottle down."

She shook her head stubbornly.

Mitch shrugged. "All right, don't put it down."

With a swift motion, he snared her raised wrist in one hand and jerked the bottle from her fingers with the other, sending wine spurting from the top. Leigh gave an anguished yelp at the sight and, with her hand still trapped in his, quickly ducked her head to survey the plush, cream-colored carpet at their feet.

"Thank God none of it spilled on my sister's carpet," she breathed, slowly bringing her gaze up past his wine-soaked shirt to meet his eyes. Then, on a giant gulp, she added, "I'm sorry I can't say the same for you."

The sight of her teeth nibbling nervously on the soft flesh of her bottom lip made Mitch want to reach out to comfort, not conquer, but with great effort he held the mutinous impulse in check. Instinctively, he knew that if he gave ground now they would be back to square one, with him making botched attempts to win her confidence and Leigh stubbornly retreating.

"Don't be sorry," he advised through clenched teeth. "I'll just add this little stunt to the list of things you owe me for."

"I owe *you* for?" she demanded, her eyes widening and turning almost violet with indignation. "May I remind you that you're the one who forced his way in here—literally—and has spent the past few days indulging his prison guard/inmate fantasies. I didn't ask for your protection then, and I don't need it now."

"Bull." Mitch strove to keep his expression coolly neutral. Actually, prison guard/inmate fantasies were about the only ones he *hadn't* been having about her, but maybe after tonight ... He forced the thought aside. "I don't much care whether you asked for my protection then or whether or not you think you need it now. As a matter of fact, what you think is totally irrelevant. The fact is, you're stuck with me, lady, for as long as I say so."

Leigh tipped her chin up and met his gaze head on. There was something flagrantly domineering about the words and the quietly aggressive tone he used to deliver them, and it occurred to her that she probably ought to feel very frightened. She didn't. She'd seen enough of the man behind the automaton who'd planted his foot in her doorway that first afternoon to rule out ever feeling that stark, frantic fear of him again. However he might enrage her or try to bully her into submission, she felt a deep certainty that Mitch would never intentionally hurt her.

"Now," he continued in that cool, modulated tone that was totally at odds with the leashed energy she could feel pulsing through him, "I think that since you were the one responsible for getting my shirt wet, you should be the one to help me take it off."

"You wouldn't need any help," she pointed out frostily, "if you'd just drop your death grip on my wrist."

His grip loosened a bit even as he shook his head. "No way. I'm in no mood to go breaking down doors to get at you after you bolt and lock yourself in your room."

Leigh released a haughty sigh. "Why on earth would I do that? I told you once before, Mitch, I'm not afraid of you."

"Maybe not," he replied as if he wasn't totally convinced. "But you're sure as hell afraid to take the risk of finding out what's happening between us."

"I know what's happening: I'm being held prisoner. What could be simpler?"

"The feelings a man and woman feel when they want each other," he countered instantly, meeting her gaze with one that withered her automatic denial before it formed. "The way you felt a little while ago when I kissed you. The way I felt the other night when your body started to come alive beneath me. That's all very simple, Leigh. And much more important than whatever reason I had for coming after you in the first place."

Leigh felt her breath drawing hard and fast, and she remained silent because she knew she couldn't deny any of it. He was right about the way she felt whenever he kissed her, touched her . . . the way she felt right now with only a whisper between her body and the lean, muscular promise of his.

"I'm right, aren't I, Leigh?" he prodded. "You are afraid of what's happening."

"No! Well, maybe." She paused and tried to harness some of the conflicting thoughts roaring through her mind. "It's just that I've never, uh—" Her head jerked up at the short, smothered sound he made, and she found him watching her with arched eyebrows and an expression of unholy amusement.

"You can wipe that look off your face," she hissed. "I didn't mean I've never been with a man before."

Mitch nodded solemnly. "Ah, a woman of vast experience."

"Maybe not so vast," she admitted uncomfortably. "In fact, the last time . . ." She lifted her eyes defiantly to his. "The *only* other time, it ended disastrously. And he didn't have half the things wrong with him that you do."

His mouth quirked. "Thanks."

"I'm sorry. I didn't mean that the way it sounded. It's just that you and I are so different."

"In all the ways that matter."

Leigh wasn't sure if he actually moved closer or if the husky, seductive pitch of his words just made her feel as if he had. Either way, his hold on her prevented her from backing away, and she was intensely aware that he'd started grazing his thumb over the soft inside of her wrist in what was unmistakably a lazy, preambling sort of caress.

"Just take our jobs for instance," she continued, trying to ignore the shivers his touch sent skittering up her arm. "I hate taking risks, and you thrive on them."

"Mmm."

"At least Joel and I had our work in common."

"Joel?" he murmured, his eyes narrowing warily, his fingers inching steadily higher on her arm.

"That was his name, Joel Haverty. He was in resort management and—"

"Fascinating. And I promise you, Leigh, that sometime soon I'm going to want to hear all about Joel Haverty and what he meant to you, but right now I think we should get back to the issue at hand: my wet shirt."

Leigh stopped breathing as he let a nerve-shattering pause develop. His eyes holding hers were overly bright, his face close enough that his warm breath anointed her skin. Slowly, he uncurled his fingers from around her wrist, freeing her.

"Take my shirt off for me, Leigh."

It was a command. Softly uttered and starkly masculine. And Leigh was powerless to resist. Her own desire to comply was too strong; her need to find out where all the sensations he set sparking inside her would lead was too compelling to be denied. Slowly, she lifted shaky fingers to the top button of his shirt and worked it loose. In the process, her fingers brushed the pelt of dark, curling hairs that covered his chest, and she felt the tingling effects of the contact spread through her like liquid fire.

With confused amazement, she realized that there was more than curiosity driving her on. Good Lord, she wanted him—in spite of the dangerous turmoil her life was in and the undeniable fact that he was not at all the sort of polite, considerate, unthreatening man she'd always planned to fall in love with. *Love*. The word danced away from the parade of others and clung insistently in her mind, driving home the fact that the past few days hadn't changed her as much as she'd first thought.

For Leigh, love and making love had always been closely linked, and it seemed they still were. That flicker of feeling out in the yard had been only a harbinger of the more insistent one winding through her now, sending her fingers tripping compliantly over the buttons of his damp shirt when every shred of common sense she possessed was telling her to run before it was too late.

It was already too late. She was falling in love with Mitch Cutter.

She kept her eyes carefully riveted on her fingers as she worked so he wouldn't read in them any evidence of her momentous discovery. Somehow she knew that Mitch wouldn't be overjoyed to learn of it. He would probably be irritated or cynically amused if she offered anything as binding or comforting as love. He certainly didn't ask for it, by word or deed, and he gave no indication that he would welcome it. But he needed it, more than any man she had ever known. Of that Leigh was absolutely certain.

She freed the final button and trembled slightly as the dark shirt fell open to reveal a broad expanse of finely muscled chest. Her eyes trailed downward, verifying what the backs of her fingers had already discerned: that the crisp black hair covering his chest turned silky as it arrowed toward his belt.

Desire, unsettlingly vivid and strong, coursed through her, and she looked up to see it reflected hotly in the swirling silver of Mitch's gaze. More than anything, she wanted to surrender to the crush of feelings drawing them together, to let the magic of his mouth and fingers override her natural restraint. At the same time, she feared that doing so might be exactly the wrong way to prove to him that he needed love, needed more than a convenient release of physical desire . . . needed her.

"Mitch, wait," she pleaded as his hands closed over hers and began dragging them toward his shoulders to finish the task they'd begun. "We should talk. This is all happening so fast, and . . . and I think we should take our time."

"There's nothing to talk about," he declared, his hands tightening on hers. "And time won't make any difference. Tonight, tomorrow, next week—this was meant to happen, Leigh. It should have happened that first night in your bed. I only wish now that it had."

"Maybe it is meant to happen," she persisted, "but this isn't the way—"

"It *is* the way," Mitch cut in roughly, releasing her hands so he could pull her body against his, letting her feel his impatience. "It's the only way I know how. By tomorrow morning you'll know you belong to me, and I'll be able to deal with this mess you're in the way I should have from the start: My way."

The words *belong to me* blazed in Leigh's mind. Surely

a man interested in only a quick tumble in bed didn't speak of the woman belonging to him in the morning. And what had he meant by *my way?* The implication didn't come as any surprise. She'd already learned that Mitch Cutter preferred to do everything his way. But what had made him say it now, when he was on the verge of making love to her? She had a sudden overwhelming urge to find out before things went any further.

"Mitch, I want to know—"

"Shhh." He bent his head and brushed her ear with the soothing sound. "You'll know everything you need to know by morning." His lips and mustache teased her ear with each husky word, sending sparks of unwanted excitement shooting through her. "You'll understand everything in the morning."

Holding her cradled against him with one arm, he lifted his fingers to the row of tiny pearl buttons along the front of her sweater. He fumbled the first two open while Leigh was still battling with the age-old instinct urging her to do as he directed, to let the questions and explanations go until morning. A few moments ago, she had been willing to give herself to him freely, with no strings attached or promises expected. She still was, but his remark about her belonging to him had teased her emotions, and Leigh longed to hear more about it.

"If this happens tonight..." she ventured shakily just as his fingers reached the fourth button.

Mitch's hand fell still, his fingers sheltered in the valley between her breasts. "If?"

The challenge in his tone was reflected in smoky eyes that followed the wave of pink Leigh felt creeping along her throat and cheeks. He finally brought his gaze back to hers just as his hand moved to close fully and possessively over her breast. "There's no *if* about it, angel.

It's already happening. But I promise you that before I'm through you'll want it every bit as much as I do."

"I—" Her admission that she thought she already did was lost in the heat of the moment as his lips opened over hers.

He held her mouth captive with the rough aggression of his kiss, seemingly lost to the fact that Leigh was a very willing participant. His tongue thrust against her lips, then swept past as they parted in welcome. He moved inside her with strong, relentless strokes, painting the roof of her mouth and the silky, sensitive inner walls with the heat and taste that was uniquely his.

The ferocity of his approach signaled that he was seeking something beyond response from her; he was bent on her surrender, on stamping her irrevocably with his seal of possession. And that knowledge filled Leigh with a rising intoxication.

There was something heady and satisfying about having the man you loved demonstrate his desire so ardently, but there was also a deeper, more elemental side to her enjoyment of Mitch's passionate assault. He wanted her in a way no other man ever had. He conveyed that fact in some unspoken, primitive way that had a spellbinding effect on Leigh's senses. The reckless passion he exuded incited the same feelings in her, unveiling a side of herself she hadn't known existed. His touch triggered yearnings she hadn't known she could feel and awakened in her sensations that were new and compelling.

Slowly, Mitch withdrew his mouth from hers and used his lips and tongue to caress a path along the side of her throat, sending small tremors of excitement racing through her body. Dark, shiny waves of hair cascaded back over her shoulders as Leigh arched her neck in response. Taking full advantage of the new territory exposed, Mitch flicked his tongue teasingly along the delicate curve of her ear until Leigh lifted her hands to his shoulders, clinging to him, shivering at the unexpected thrill that shot through her.

With a low, supremely satisfied groan, Mitch intensified his efforts, first bathing her ear with a warm, swirling tongue, then filling it with a steamy mist that seemed to waft all through her in heated waves. When he finally shifted again, this time to nibble at the curve of her shoulder while he resumed work on her buttons, Leigh found herself leaning against his sinewy length for support as a sense of weakness seeped through her.

Wanting to share the pleasure washing over her, she slowly began to emulate the way his hands were moving over her body. Her caresses were hesitant at first, and at first Mitch didn't quite seem to get the message that his seize-and-conquer approach had long ceased being necessary. Finally, when she curled her fingers around the edges of his open shirt and slid it off his shoulders, her message of willingness seemed to pierce his dazed senses. Jerking his head up as she determinedly lowered the shirt along his arms and let it drift to the floor, he stared at her with eyes full of astonishment.

"You aren't fighting me," he whispered.

A small smile, as old as woman, curved Leigh's lips. "No. Would you rather I did?"

"No." His head shook in a somewhat hazy echo of the reply. Then understanding and relief flickered across his face before a look of scorching intent settled there once more. "Hell no, I don't want you to fight me, woman. I want you to give yourself to me freely. I want all the softness and warmth I know I'll find waiting inside you for me. I want to bury myself in your softness. I told you before, I want to lose myself in you."

"But the last time you said it, you didn't look so sure it was what you really wanted."

He caged her face with his hands and met her searching gaze with one that held all the passion and strength she would ever need. "I'm sure. And I promise that before the night is over, you'll be just as sure . . . and you'll never be sorry."

He parted his lips while Leigh watched, mesmerized, on fire with expectation. Then slowly he lowered his mouth to hers. His kiss was at once lighter and more riveting than any that had gone before. He made her lips wet and slippery with moisture from his own, then slid over them with whisper-light contact while his fingers peeled open the front of her sweater until his naked chest was melded to hers.

His skin felt hot and rough against her smoothness, and the intimacy of the contact made the restrained, wet, open-mouthed movements of his lips on hers seem suddenly intensely erotic . . . and then unbearably unsatisfying. Heedless of the low, throaty chuckle her action inspired, Leigh wove her fingers through his hair and anchored her lips to his with the firm, grinding pressure he had made her crave. She let her tongue move over his lips, gasping slightly at her first taste of the dark, velvet recesses beyond.

With a jagged sound of desire Mitch slid his hands from her shoulders to her buttocks, pulling her firmly into the spread of his legs while he began to move against her in a slow, suggestive body caress. Leigh quickly picked up the rhythm with her tongue, using it to set the pace as she learned all the sleek and rough textures that were his, following as he gradually increased the tempo in pressure and urgency.

Finally, when she didn't know how much more she

could take of this teasing prelude to what they both wanted, he used his hold on her to put some distance between their straining bodies, emitting a muffled, frustrated groan as he did so.

"Slow down," he ordered between fractured breaths. "I've been wanting this for so long . . . I think I'm about at my breaking point."

Leigh lowered thick, sooty lashes over suddenly shy eyes and whispered, "I think I'm about there, too."

With a light touch beneath her chin, Mitch tipped her face up to his. The smile on his lips was enchanted and adoring, scattering whatever residual traces of resistance might have stood between Leigh and the world of wonder and sensation he promised with every touch of his lips, every sweep of his hand.

"In that case," he said, drawing her closer to the fire burning in the fireplace behind him, "maybe you'd be more comfortable over here."

As she stepped obediently around him, Mitch bent to turn off the lamp, haphazardly tossing two pillows from the sofa onto the floor in the process. Then he turned to face her once more.

"Thank you for admitting you're as ready as I am," he said, a hint of self-deprecation coloring his low-pitched drawl. "I wasn't sure how much longer I could hold off."

Almost desperately, he reached out and tugged her against him, pressing her face close to his chest, letting her hair tumble over his arms like shiny black satin streamers. "Oh, Leigh . . . angel," he breathed raspily, "let me love you . . . let me prove to you that I can be the man you want . . . the man of your dreams."

Leigh's slight, silent nod against his chest was all it took to send Mitch's hands roving down her spine, along the back of her thighs and up again in a wild, hungry caress. They came to rest finally on the ruffled collar of her sweater. Slowly he inched it over her shoulders and along her arms until it fell in a soft, pale heap beside his shirt.

Leaning back, he said simply, "You're beautiful."

It was more than enough. His eyes were on fire, praising her more eloquently than a thousand sonnets could.

Lightly he let his palms coast up over her ribs, following the curve of her breasts, brushing the rose-hued tips that were already puckered from the potency of his gaze alone.

"Your skin is like ivory," he marveled, touching her reverently with his long, sensitive fingers. His voice was husky and distracted. "I never knew ivory could feel so warm . . . so soft . . . so womanly. My woman," he finished with a fevered groan as he jerked her against him.

Leigh surrendered to his supple strength, nestling against him, feeling very much at home. His explicit approval was like another torch held to her already overheated senses, and it was with heady anticipation that she felt his fingers move to the snap of her jeans. He flicked it open and lowered the zipper with mounting impatience, then dragged the worn, soft fabric down her legs, lavishing caresses on her thighs and calves as he went. Her socks and lace-edged panties quickly followed, and then Mitch was sweeping her up in his arms and lowering her gently to the soft carpeting below.

He gazed down at her, mesmerized, for a long time. Then Leigh felt the desire in his gaze melt something untouched deep inside her, and her own hunger was recharged in a heated gush. She lifted her arms to him in an instinctive plea.

"Mitch, please," she whispered, "I need you . . . now."

Holding her gaze, he artlessly unfastened his jeans

and stepped out of them and his underwear at once. Leigh drew a breath in sharply and held it as he stretched out beside her with loose-limbed grace. The firelight sent shadows dancing over his skin, gilding its bronze surface with a golden glow that highlighted the taut planes and fascinating swells of muscle. She was suddenly overcome by the need to touch all of him, to learn the shape and texture of him as intimately as she knew her own. But when she reached out, he caught both her wrists in one hand and held her arms stretched high over her head.

"Lie still," he whispered, invitation and insistence tangled in the husky command.

Leigh responded willingly to both, lying as still as she possibly could while he touched her first with a gaze that was starkly possessive, then with the slow-moving fingers of his free hand. He feathered an intricate pattern of sensation along her throat and the arch of her breasts, coaxing them to full, aching arousal. He coasted over her ribs, lingering at the hollow of her waist, then playing across the flat, silky plane of her stomach with maddening lassitude.

Leigh arched in reflex as his fingertips skirted the triangle of soft, curling hair just below. Watching her with total absorption, Mitch let out a deep-chested sound of satisfaction. Smiling down at her, he moved on to her thighs, gently parting them, painting delicate designs on the insides that made her strain against the hand anchoring hers firmly above her head. He refused to bow to her flexing muscles and the small, muffled sounds she made urging him to stray closer to the heart of her desire. He acted as if there were all the time in the world and he planned to use every second of it for the sole purpose of bringing her pleasure.

Finally, when Leigh didn't think she could live through

another instant of such pleasure unless he touched her—
really touched her—he did. Freeing her hands so they
could curl around his neck, he lowered his mouth to hers
in a long, searching kiss as his fingers gently explored
her in a way no man ever had.

His touch was magic, creating delicious, tingling sensations that intensified and splintered as she clung to his
shoulders, her head turned to the side, her breathing
becoming thick and rapid as he slowly, patiently brought
her to the border of her own physical experience and
beyond. Gradually, the speed and pressure of his touch
intensified, and with it the purity of her body's response.

"Let it happen, angel," he urged hoarsely. "Just let it
happen. I'm here and I'll keep you safe . . . always."

Leigh opened her eyes, and at that moment her world
began and ended with the touch of his fingers and his
face above her, dark and masculine and etched with tenderness. All feeling suddenly seemed centered in the part
of her he was stroking closer and closer to the brink of
climax.

When it came it was with the force of a shock wave,
lifting Leigh's hips off the floor and driving her legs
together as everything inside seemed to explode into
thousands of shimmering sparks that slowly drifted back
down to cover her like a blanket of warm contentment.

Mitch gazed down at her tightly closed eyes and gently
heaving chest with a feeling of utter satisfaction and
relief. He had wanted to satisfy her fully, and it thrilled
him to know he'd been able to. He had told himself that
satisfying her physically was an integral part of creating
this bond between them, a bond that would be strong
and compelling enough to make her trust him. But he
knew it went even beyond that.

Somehow, he'd known that tonight his own fulfillment was inexplicably linked to hers. Oh, he had no doubt that he would achieve physical release in her arms— probably in an embarrassingly brief time if the ache in his loins was any barometer. Fear of just how brief it might be had kept him from trying to satisfy her *after* their bodies were joined. That was a risk he felt heavily weighted against him tonight. He'd spent too many hours lately anticipating this moment to think he could proceed with even a normal amount of stamina.

No, it wasn't his physical satisfaction that hinged on hers; it was emotional. And until tonight he hadn't believed there was such a thing as deriving emotional satisfaction from the sex act. Not for him anyway. Now he not only knew it existed; he was experiencing it. And it made him willing to wait until Leigh reached for him again before satisfying the hunger still pulsing inside him.

He didn't have to wait long. Her thick lashes fluttered, then lifted to reveal eyes that gleamed blue-black with contentment. Mitch felt another surge of satisfaction that rapidly crystallized into something much more urgent as she slid closer and placed one hand tentatively on his chest.

"Am I allowed to touch you now?" she asked, her smile teasing and bewitching.

"Yes." He cleared his throat against the telltale rasp that had invaded his voice and added, "Any time."

"Good. I choose now." The tips of her fingers outlined his shoulders, tracing a tendon the length of his inner arm and back. "You feel good," she whispered. "Hard, muscular . . . do you lift weights?"

"No." He felt the nerves across the top of his chest

tremble as she touched him there and wondered if she felt it, too—if she knew the power she had over him at this moment.

"I'm glad," she said, leaving him wondering what the hell she was glad about until she added, "Men who lift weights always seem to bulge. I like your arms and chest so much better."

She ran her fingers over him as she spoke, ending with a swirling caress that dipped down to his stomach, making the muscles there quiver, then clench. God, was she going to drag this out forever? he anguished. She was tormenting him. The way you did her, a small voice intruded. Only then it hadn't seemed like torment, but pleasure—a soaring variety he'd never experienced before, one he'd wished could go on forever.

Leaning against him, she reached around to his back, working her fingers enticingly along his spine. Mitch let his head drop to her shoulder, tasting the salty sheen left there from his loving, smelling the light scent of wild flowers that clung to her always. She filled his senses until he felt the urge to tumble her backward grow stronger than his powers of restraint. He was about to make his move when her soft voice forced him to rein in his desire once more.

"Mitch, what's this?" she asked softly.

Damn. He felt her fingers resting cautiously just below his left shoulder blade. He knew what she felt there— the ridge of scar tissue, the puckered flesh around it, souvenirs of a careless night he couldn't afford to forget.

"It's nothing," he replied, drawing her hand back to his chest. "An accident I can hardly remember anymore."

"But—"

"Shhh. Just hold me, Leigh. I need you . . . and I want you." He buried his face in the warmth of her neck and breathed deeply. "God, how I want you."

As if the admission of his need and desire gave her courage, her playfulness ceased and her caresses became more earnest, the instinctive movements of a woman seeking to please her man. She stroked his chest with her palms and her tongue, making him groan and call up every mind trick he knew to hold off long enough to give her time to learn his body the way he had hers.

She touched his hips and thighs, feathered the tensed surface of his stomach lingeringly. As she ventured lower, her movements grew steadily slower, more cautious. And the threads of Mitch's control wound steadily tighter. Finally, she brushed the rigid manifestation of his desire with the back of her fingertips, and the breath Mitch had been holding in eager anticipation exploded in a frenzied rush. He groaned and trembled. Leigh froze.

"No," he growled when she began to ease her hand away. "Don't stop, please. I've waited so long to feel you touch me. Please, angel, touch me."

He waited in agony for her response. Slowly, she lifted her head and smiled at him. Her smile was more dazzling than ever in the glow of the fire, and it unlocked doors to places inside Mitch that had never been touched before.

"I love touching you," she said softly, "but I'm not sure I know how to please you."

"I am," he broke in firmly. "Surer than I've ever been about anything."

With the smile still playing about her lips, she slowly turned her hand until her palm was cupping him gently.

"You feel hot," she whispered in a voice touched with awe. "Hot satin."

"Oh, God," Mitch moaned, thrusting against the smooth warmth of her hand as her fingers closed possessively around him. He had wanted her to touch him, not knowing the firebolts of desire it would send arcing through him or the way the silky contact would push his hunger for her past the point where he could control it.

A little desperately, mumbling disjointed phrases of need and apology, he pressed her back to the carpet. The need to take her, to make her his, surged inside him, but an even stronger instinct gentled his movements as he brought his body down on top of hers and used his knee to urge her thighs apart.

Leigh heeded his silent commands eagerly, with a responsiveness that fueled his need to possess her. His body blocked the firelight from hers, and in the shadows she looked to Mitch like the essence of femininity: mysterious and welcoming and everything he needed to make him whole. He could resist no longer.

He moved to bury himself in her softness, and Leigh cried out at the full thrust of his possession. Mitch froze above her slender frame until he realized that it was a cry of passion, not pain, and that her arms were already reaching for him, seeking to pull him closer, deeper.

In that instant, he knew that he would never get enough of her, of the way she surrounded him like a sea of flaming liquid, of the small sounds of wonder that came from deep in her throat, of the way she turned his name into a husky caress as she arched to meet him in passion.

Leigh Bramwell was his forever.

The thought stayed with him even as he surrendered control with an exultant, half-stifled cry and collapsed on top of her in a dark world of rippling after-shocks. He felt like a man who had just lost himself . . . and found something much more precious instead.

Afterward, he lay in silence, thinking about the perfection of the woman curled close to his side and about the subtle incongruities in her that he would probably never fully understand. Like how for all the fragility he sensed in her nature, when push came to shove, she'd had the strength to admit her desire for him without coyness. And how she managed to respond in a way that was at once magnificently proud and subtly submissive.

He didn't care if he never understood it. All that mattered was that she was perfect for him. And she was his. If he had worried beforehand that Leigh might not realize just how fully and irrevocably she was surrendering to him tonight, he didn't now. There was no way a woman could give herself to a man with the abandon and sweetness she just had and not realize that she was binding herself to him in a way that transcended all else.

And that in the process she was handing over to him certain undeniable rights. Like the right to protect his woman. And the right to know exactly what the hell he was protecting her from. Rights that Mitch planned to start exercising first thing in the morning.

Chapter Six

MITCH HAD DECIDED to wait until morning because he thought Leigh would be too worn out to do much talking or explaining tonight. Then she tipped her head back and peered up at him with eyes that were drowsily content and faintly curious.

"Mitch?" she said softly, her breath ruffling the hair on his chest.

"Hmm?"

"What sort of accident was it?"

"What accident?" His expression tensed as he answered the question himself before she had a chance to. Keeping his voice carefully neutral, he asked, "You mean the scar?"

"Yes."

Mitch intercepted the hand she lifted to touch that spot on his back and carried it to his lips instead, licking her fingertips and nuzzling the small pad of flesh at the base of her thumb, stalling while he struggled to restore some order to his love-sated mind. He wouldn't lie to her about the scar, but he also knew he had to shade the truth to protect the lie he'd already told. A lie that had to stand until he'd found out what he needed to know about her involvement with DeMarco. He fully expected she would be a little piqued when she first discovered that he wasn't exactly what he'd claimed to be, and he couldn't chance letting her mood get in the way of what he had to do.

"It happened about five years ago," he explained carefully. "I got a little careless on one of my first assignments and turned my back on the wrong woman."

"You mean one of your first assignments as a federal agent?"

"Mmm." It was the most noncommittal sound he could manage.

"Who was the woman?"

"The wife of a man running an interstate car theft ring. I tracked him to his brother's house and went in to get him. He was no problem, but when we were walking out his loving wife picked up a letter opener and buried it in my back." He felt Leigh flinch in his arms, and he ran his hand soothingly along the swell of her hip. "It won't ever happen again; I still carry the blade they dug out of me as a reminder not to turn my back on anyone."

"There are other ways to get hurt besides turning your back on someone," she asserted quietly.

Mitch flashed her a knowing grin. "Yeah, like crossing the street or driving on the freeway at rush hour."

"I think I liked you better when you didn't joke," she grumbled, pressing closer with an unspoken message of concern that was all new to him. "Your job is dangerous, Mitch."

"Life is dangerous."

"Don't. I don't think I'll be able to stand it if you're so damn casual about it, about the fact that every time you go on an assignment you could get hurt . . . or worse."

"Not every time. Take this assignment for instance." He swept his hand from her hip to her breast and back slowly. "This is what's known as a real soft job."

She reluctantly gave in to the smile playing about her lips. "Well, I'm just glad they sent you and not the two nice fatherly types who came to my house that day."

"And I'm glad you didn't succumb to their nice fatherly charm and cheat me of the chance to come up here and, uh, interrogate you myself."

She arched her neck for his kiss. "Me too. I'd much rather succumb to your bossy arrogant sort of charm."

All Mitch's instincts as a hunter told him that the moment was right to tighten the velvet chains around her. Winding his hand in her hair, he tipped her face up, tethering her gaze with the intensity of his own.

"Then do it," he urged, trying hard to sound persuasive rather than demanding. "Succumb."

She giggled. "You're not paying attention—I just did."

His smile was forced, a smokescreen to conceal the fact that he was no longer feeling playful. "But I want you to surrender your mind along with your body. Tell me about you and DeMarco, Leigh."

She didn't stiffen, and the guarded expression he dreaded didn't subdue the deep blue sparkle in her eyes. She simply yawned and dropped her head back to his chest.

"I'm too sleepy," she mumbled. "I'll tell you in the morning."

"In the morning you might not find my bossy arrogance half as charming. Tell me now, angel." When she responded only with a sleepy, wiggling protest that threatened to distract him, he prodded, "You must have needed money to buy the inn, and—"

That prompted a definite shake of her head even before he'd finished the thought. "Not to buy it," she corrected firmly. "There's no way I ever would have gotten involved in the whole thing in the first place if I hadn't thought I could afford it."

He remembered her abhorrence of taking risks, and a smile tugged at his mouth. "Of course, the ever cautious angel. But even angels can miscalculate, and when you came up short of enough cash to cinch the deal, you turned to DeMarco."

"I didn't miscalculate," she insisted, indignation lifting her voice from the sleepy cadence it had held. "I was misled."

"By whom?"

Her hands fluttered expansively. "Everybody. The electrician, the plumber, the carpenter—even the woman who made the damn drapes."

Her hands settled back in the comfortable nook between their bodies, but Mitch could tell she was roused and willing. All he had to do was let her tell it at her own pace.

"I had enough money from my savings, plus a hefty contribution from my folks, to handle the down payment and all the renovations necessary to make the inn meet the codes for public accommodations. And Mark introduced me to a friend of his who helped me get a loan from the Small Business Association for the rest."

"Mark. The chef," Mitch remarked dryly. He was feeling an instinctive dislike for this man who was friendly enough with Leigh to help with such an important business deal. "Is he by any chance the same friend who's looking after your place while you're away?"

"He's not looking after it really, just handling some of the final renovations that I couldn't reschedule." She flicked him a curious glance. "How did you know about that?"

"It's my job."

"Well, at least you're good at it," she sighed. "That's more than I can say. This deal with the inn seemed like such a safe venture at first, too."

"So what went wrong?"

"Everything. When the actual work began, we discovered that the updating was going to be more comprehensive—and costly—than I'd planned on. Much more costly. I ended up needing new electrical wiring and paying a premium for copper pipes to match the original ones and—"

"Copper pipes to match the original ones?" He raked his hand through his hair in irritation and impatience. "Didn't anybody check the estimates and job specs before the work began?"

"I did."

Feeling her defensive stiffening, he took a deep breath before asking, "What about Mr. Helpful?"

"You mean Mark?" She shrugged. "He doesn't really know much more about all that than I do."

A rush of pure male satisfaction moved through him. "Well, I do," he told her. "And from now on I'll handle all that for you. Just like I'm going to handle DeMarco. Now tell me the rest."

Leigh sighed. "It's pretty simple . . . and pretty stupid. I used the money I'd put aside for things like linen and china and food staples to pay the overages on the repair work. I figured I had a little time to try to get an increase in my SBA loan before I actually had to buy the supplies, and as a last resort I knew I could always borrow the money from my sister."

Mitch wasn't sure if the shiver he felt in her was from nerves or the chill settling over the room as the fire died. Reaching for the embroidered quilt draped across the back of the chair beside him, he arranged it over both of them.

"Go on," he urged quietly, pulling her back into his arms.

"One night when I was out with Vinnie, I ended up telling him about the problems I was having. He suggested it would be lot easier and less embarrassing if he just arranged for a little cash advance from a good friend of his." Her voice took on a shade of self-disgust. "He said I could pay it back at the going interest rate once the inn was making a profit."

Mitch rubbed his chin against the top of her head. "Sounds like a great deal. Except the friend turned out to be a loan shark . . . and not so friendly."

Leigh nodded. "Even Vinnie turned out to be more of a louse than a friend. He was only being so helpful so I would . . ."

"Succumb?" Mitch supplied more calmly than the thought left him feeling.

"That's one way of putting it," she agreed with a shudder. "And on top of that, he was using my reason for needing the loan to cover for one he wanted for himself. He had plans to buy into some big drug deal, and he was afraid DeMarco would turn him down flat if he told him the truth."

"That's right. That would be too risky for a loan shark to touch."

"I guess it *was* risky, because the deal fell through,

and Vinnie lost out on the big killing he was going to make. He wanted to use that money to repay DeMarco. He'd had it all so well planned, too. Once he paid off DeMarco, I would be left owing *him* the money. I can see now that he hoped I'd be grateful enough to—" She broke off with a small shrug. "Anyway, about a week after I'd already spent most of my part of the money, he called and told me that *we* had to come up with twenty thousand dollars in three days."

Her laughter held a note of panic that tore at Mitch's heartstrings. He wished Vinnie and DeMarco were there now, so he could deal with them while the memory of her trembling was still raw in his mind.

"And that's the first you knew of where the money had really come from?"

"Of course. Do you think I'm stupid enough to get myself in hock to a loan shark for twenty thousand dollars when I only saw three of it?"

"Honey, I think that's exactly what you did."

With a defeated groan she sank against his chest. "If only I'd trusted my instinct *not* to trust Vinnie."

"Why didn't you? Was he arrogantly charming, too?"

"Jealous?"

The affectionately mocking taunt hit closer to home than he felt comfortable with. "Should I be?"

"No."

His hold tightened in response to her generous honesty.

"Mitch, I told you the truth about Vinnie," she continued. "We'd been dating for a while, but we never..." She faltered awkwardly, charmingly. "It was nothing like this. I've never felt anything like this before."

"Nothing has ever been like this for me either," he

admitted quietly. "I'm glad you feel the same way. I want you happy as well as safe. You're mine, Leigh."

He coiled his leg tightly around hers, reiterating his claim on her. If she didn't yet understand the full magnitude of what had transpired between them, he would have to instruct her in it now. But she didn't protest or argue; she simply nuzzled against him once more. This time her sigh had a drowsy, acquiescent tone that danced across his flesh like lightning. Mitch closed his eyes, knowing the problem was far from resolved but satisfied that at least she understood how completely she had given herself over to his care.

Now if she would only react with the same trusting sweetness to the news that he was actually a bounty hunter who had agreed to track her down for five thousand dollars.

Leigh woke the next morning tucked snugly into the double bed in the master bedroom. The pillow angled close to hers bore the imprint of the man who'd carried her there late last night. Smiling, she reached out and traced it with her fingertip. So it wasn't just a dream.

She grinned at that. Just a few days ago, the idea of being ravished by Mitch Cutter would have seemed like a nightmare. Now here she was, waking up slightly sore and a little sorry that he was such a chronically early riser. How on earth had he managed to slip past all her defenses in just three days? She had no idea, and, curling her arms around his pillow, she decided she didn't care. All that mattered was that she had been right to take the monumental risk she'd taken last night.

There had been a real, flesh and blood man inside the government robot after all. A man who was deeply sensual and not afraid to show that he needed her as much as she needed him. Leigh felt closer to Mitch than she ever had to anyone in her whole life. And she was glad she had told him everything. She knew he would do whatever he could to help her out of this mess without getting her embroiled in an even bigger one with the government in the process. He might still be on the case officially, but she was certain last night had changed his priorities just as it had hers. They would work things out. Together.

Mitch strode into the room a minute later carrying a mug of hot coffee. His hair was still damp from the shower, and he was dressed in jeans and the yellow shirt he'd bought on their trip to the mall. To Leigh the shirt seemed the touching symbol of a surrender as portentous as the one she had made hours ago. It signified his understanding of the new bond between them.

"Good morning," she said as he lowered the cup to the nightstand and leaned over to kiss her with easy intimacy. "You're up even earlier than usual."

"I'm afraid you're going to have to get up earlier than usual, too," he replied in the deep, no-nonsense voice that had been so gentle in passion. "I want to get an early start."

Without any real reason, other than his return to a cool, unemotional demeanor, an uneasy feeling crept over Leigh. "Start for where?"

Mitch's face registered mild surprise. "Home, of course. There's no reason to hang around here any longer."

Turning abruptly, he crossed the room and disappeared into the bathroom, leaving Leigh struggling to find some explanation for his behavior—other than the most obvious one. Last night he had managed to demolish her wall of resistance and find out all he needed to know in the process, and now his job was finished. Mission accomplished.

Gathering the sheet in front of her, she sat up and

noticed what she hadn't seen before. Her suitcase was propped open on the chair across the room, and the clothes she'd left scattered about had been piled into it in a rather haphazard fashion. Rage began to build in her gradually at the sheer audacity and total lack of subtlety he was displaying. Her anger had just reached the cool, brittle stage when Mitch emerged from the bathroom carrying her brush and cosmetics case.

An indulgent smile tipped his mouth as he glanced at her. "C'mon, honey, you really have to get up, especially if you want a shower before we take off." Eyebrows lowering, he held up the cosmetics case. "I guess maybe I should have left this where it was until you're through dressing."

"Maybe. And while you're at it, why don't you just put the rest of my things back where I had them and explain to me why you took the liberty of moving them in the first place?" She squared her shoulders. "But then, maybe you think last night gave you the right to take whatever liberties you choose?"

Mitch had frozen at the bite in her tone. Now she watched a look of relief sweep away the guarded concern with which he'd been regarding her.

"Is that all that's bothering you?" he asked with a twist of amusement that was very unwise. "Honey, I know it must seem as if I'm taking you for granted, and I know a woman likes to be pampered a little the morning after, but I just don't have time for it this morning."

His cavalier attitude appalled her. "Well, it just so happens you don't know as much about women as you think. I *don't* like being pampered," she snarled, "any more than I like being *used* by a cold-hearted bastard who'll stop at nothing to get his damn job done."

From across the room she could almost feel the wave of shock that rocked his hard body.

"What the hell are you talking about?" he demanded coldly.

"About last night!" Leigh raged. "About the way you lied and turned all sneaky, snakelike charming so I'd tell you what you were sent here to find out. Well, now you know. I did borrow money from DeMarco, and I don't have it to pay him back, so I'll probably end up cooperating with your damn investigation. You won." She swept at the disheveled hair tumbling around her face with her free hand. "So what now, Mitch? A bonus? A promotion? I hope whatever it is, it's worth the sacrifice of screwing a loser like me."

Tubes of mascara and lipstick scattered as he hurled the case away with a violent oath. Then he was across the room, one knee slamming into the mattress as he gripped her shoulders, his expression tight-lipped and ominous.

"Stop it!" he growled. "That's not the way it was, and you know it."

"I know that that's exactly the way it was."

He seemed to be tottering on the edge of an explosion, and Leigh wondered briefly if she'd also been wrong about his being unable to hurt her. Jerking his hands from her shoulders, he held them stiffly in front of him, as if he was wondering along the same lines. When he spoke, his voice was unnaturally quiet, throbbing with tension.

"Leigh, I don't have time for these feminine hysterics this morning. I want you to get—"

"Feminine hysterics?" she gasped in disbelief. "And I suppose a man in my position would simply say 'Thank you for making a fool of me, oh, by the way, did you remember to pack the toothbrush?' "

He lurched from the bed and gaped down at her, looking more harried than angry. Or maybe that was just as close to looking guilty as his callous type ever came, she thought maliciously.

"Okay, Leigh," he began slowly. "I'm going to try to start over and explain this to you the way I probably should have when I first walked in here." He shrugged confusedly. "I guess I just thought you would understand. The reason we're leaving here this morning is so that I can take care of this thing with DeMarco for you."

"Sure, by turning me over to your superiors."

"Will you shut up? I'm not going to turn you over to anybody. You're mine now, Leigh. It's my responsibility to protect you, and I'm going to do it."

That announcement sort of crimped the gears of her great theory on how he'd seduced her in the line of duty. But it didn't explain why he was back to acting like her master this morning instead of her lover and her friend. What had happened to the man who'd treated her with such tenderness last night? The man she thought would be her ally in this, a man who would understand and work with her to put all this behind them?

One thing was certain: He was not the man standing over her now, looking as though he wished he'd packed her safely away with the shirts and sweaters before she woke up and became troublesome. How could she have been so wrong about him?

"Don't look so pensive, Leigh," he ordered. "It's much too late for second thoughts."

"About what?"

"About giving yourself to me."

"I didn't!" she hissed furiously.

"You sure did. Sweetly, too."

"That was sex."

"Uh-uh. It was a commitment. One I intend to honor."

"Have fun! You'll be honoring the most one-sided commitment in history."

"I don't think so," he countered without a trace of irritation or uncertainty. "I intend to see that you honor it as well. And I don't think that will be much of a problem once I get this thing with DeMarco settled. It's got you pretty jittery."

"You've got me pretty jittery," she growled. "I think you're crazy."

His mouth twisted into a rueful grin. "I think maybe you're right. Why else would I be standing here arguing a moot point when I've got a long list of other things to attend to? Starting with paying a visit to our friend Eddie DeMarco."

"DeMarco?" she echoed. "Why?"

"To explain to him that you are not indebted to him for the sum of twenty thousand dollars and to convince him that it's to your mutual advantage that the amount you do owe him be canceled."

"Ha! Right. He's really going to agree to that."

Mitch ran his palm over his beard, a smug sort of smile playing about his lips. "I think he and I can come to terms."

Leigh rolled her eyes in disgust. "He's a loan shark for godsake. The only terms they understand are cash."

"Too bad you didn't remember that earlier."

"And even if he does agree, what then?" she challenged. "Are you going to convince your boss that it's to his advantage to forget I was ever a potential witness in the first place?"

Shrugging, he lifted her robe from the bottom of the bed and dropped it on her. "Something along that line.

But first I have to get you safely stowed away back at your place. Now would you like to get dressed and drive your own car back to Rhode Island? Or shall I just throw you in the back of the Jeep as you are?"

For a second, she measured the steely determination in his eyes. Then she uttered tersely, "I'll get dressed."

Under the fire of her glare, Mitch grudgingly conceded to turn his back while she shrugged into the robe and stood to belt it tightly. When she went to step around him on her way to the bathroom, he reached out and touched her arm hesitantly.

"Leigh . . ."

"Don't!" she snapped, jerking away from the contact. "I don't want you touching me. Not after what happened last night."

"What happened last night is going to happen again," he vowed with more than a hint of impatience. "And if you're honest, you'll admit you want it as much as I do—as much as you wanted it last night."

"Last night I thought you were someone I could trust," she countered, her voice suddenly halting.

She pressed the back of her hand to her stinging eyes, and it came away wet. The sight seemed to disturb Mitch even more than her wrath had.

"You can trust me, angel," he said grimly.

"Don't call me that," Leigh forced through gritted teeth. "And don't try to tell me that making love to me last night wasn't simply the quickest, surest way of accomplishing what you were sent here to do."

"It was more than that," he insisted, taking a step toward her and stopping in frustration when she skittered away.

"And what if it hadn't been?" she challenged. "You're so hell-bent on protecting me, what if it had come down to the fact that the only way you could find out what you needed to know was to seduce me? Would you have done it? For my own protection, of course."

Mitch made deep furrows in his hair with his fingers. "That—"

"Would you have?" she demanded.

He met her gaze with a look of grim resignation, like a man with his back to the wall. "Yes. If that was the only way, yes. But—"

"That's all I wanted to know."

"Leigh!" he called sharply as she whirled and ran to the bathroom. "Leigh, dammit, I'm not through talking to you. I want to explain . . ."

He was still bellowing when Leigh turned on the water full force, the roar of it blotting the sound of him out of her life. At least for a little while.

An hour later Mitch pounded the leather-wrapped steering wheel of the Jeep with his fist and cursed himself for the hundredth time since he'd started following Leigh's car along this southbound route home. How had he managed to screw things up so totally this morning? The answer was obvious. He just wasn't used to dealing with another person on a day-to-day basis this way. And he sure wasn't used to explaining his every move and including someone else when he was making plans the way Leigh obviously expected him to.

Glaring at the rear bumper of her car, feeling extremely maligned and frustrated, he uttered an impassioned oath about women in general. Hell, was it too much to expect her to be pleased—maybe even a little grateful—that he was taking things in hand so efficiently? After all, he'd lain awake half the night analyzing all the possible angles he could take and deciding the best one was to approach DeMarco head on and handle the Feds by tossing them good old Vinnie as a witness in lieu of his woman. No doubt Vinnie would have a lot more to talk about, anyway. And if they couldn't convince him he ought to talk, Mitch would. He'd always been creative in that department, and one of the nice things about not being bound by anyone else's rules and codes of behavior was that he had free rein to indulge it.

He probably should have dressed this all up into a nice, neat battle plan and laid it out for Leigh while she sipped her coffee. Maybe then she wouldn't have jumped to this half-baked conclusion that he'd only made love to her to get her to talk. That was a part of the truth, but not all of it—not by a long shot. He had tried to make that clear to her both last night and this morning by telling her that protecting her was a right he had claimed when he made her his, not a job he could walk away from when it was over. Obviously, he hadn't made it clear enough, or she wouldn't have stormed out of the bathroom and off to her car without saying another word to him.

The only bright spot in the whole morning so far was that her contemptuous silence had at least prevented him from doing what he'd steeled himself to do: reveal that it was at Eddie DeMarco's bidding that he'd come after her originally. He had already hurt her, and he would have to live with the sight of her tears for a long time. He wasn't about to add panic to her pain and maybe push her into doing something stupid like running away again. He already had his hands full without chasing her all over New England.

He would simply wait to tell her about that part of it until he'd redeemed himself a little by sorting out her more immediate problems. Not that he was stupid enough to think that championing her cause was going to completely atone for lying to her at the start. She would be angry all right. But in the end she would give him another chance. Mitch felt certain of that. She was just too soft and gentle not to.

When they arrived at the inn in Jamestown, Mitch left her with a scant explanation of where he was headed and strict orders not to leave home or let anyone in until he returned. Leigh didn't argue. She had decided during the long drive back that passive resistance was probably the best tack to use in dealing with his type. A nice theory, but a little tough to stick with, she discovered, when someone of his type pinned you against your front door and demanded a violent, love-grinding kiss farewell.

The kiss left her embarrassed about her own easy arousal at his hands and doubting her earlier insistence that his *only* reason for making love to her had been professional. Sipping a cup of tea in the spacious, airy kitchen at the back of the house, she thought about the slow, intense way he had loved her. She remembered his patience and tenderness and the magical way he had sent her soaring to new heights of ecstasy and then enfolded her in the security of his arms afterward. She considered the way genuine concern and anger had flickered in his voice and his eyes as she'd unfolded her story. Then slowly, cautiously, she approached the idea that she might have been wrong this morning.

Not that he had been so all-fired right. Packing her things and ordering her around as if he had a right to do so. Just remembering it made her scowl through the bow window at the waves rushing to shore on the beach out back. So maybe he was right about not wasting any more time before seeing DeMarco. He had still handled the situation pretty poorly. But then, she vacillated, maybe she had, too. It was hard to know how to react when he turned all cool and monosyllabic that way. She'd never met anyone quite like Mitch before. Her lips curved in wry amusement as it occurred to her that he probably hadn't met anyone quite like her before, either.

No doubt there were women in his past—quite a few if his level of amorous skill was any indication. But something told Leigh that he'd never had to deal with any of them outside of a bedroom before. That until now he'd never wanted to. The notion pleased her immensely.

Her first thought when the front doorbell rang a few hours later was that Mitch had returned, and she still wasn't exactly sure how she felt about it—in spite of the defiant leap of excitement her heart gave. Setting aside the razor she'd been using to scrape specks of paint off the windows, she sauntered to the front door with a calm air that she hoped hid her true feelings.

But it was not Mitch's Jeep parked in the circular front drive; it was the nondescript green sedan Leigh recognized from the afternoon the first two federal agents had come calling. Wondering why they were here instead of Mitch and determined not to give one more inch until she knew exactly where she stood with all of them, she released the catch and swung open the small eye-level window in the front door.

"Good afternoon, Ms. Bramwell." The taller of the two graying, middle-aged men greeted her with a professional smile. "Maybe you remember us—"

"I remember," she broke in curtly, causing both men to drop their smiles.

"Good. We dropped by earlier this week to see if you'd thought over our suggestions concerning your rather dangerous situation with Edward DeMarco. You must have been out of town."

The polite question in his remark strained Leigh's patience. "Yes, I was out of town, and you know it. And I'm not going to stand here and play whatever little game you're playing. I've said all I plan to say to your cohort, so you can go harass him for whatever you want to know."

"Excuse me, Ms. Bramwell," the second man spoke up as she began to swing the window shut. "I'm not sure what cohort you're referring to. Dan here and I have been working alone on this aspect of the case."

"Right," she scoffed, "and I'm J. Edgar Hoover's long-lost granddaughter. Look, I know you're working with someone else because I just had the dubious pleasure of spending three days in his protective custody."

The men exchanged bland looks that started apprehension curling inside Leigh.

"I see," the tall man said. "Did you happen to get the name of this man?"

Rolling her eyes in disgust, she snapped, "No, I spent three days alone with a total stranger!" Abruptly, it occurred to Leigh that that wasn't so far from the truth. In a more subdued tone, she said, "His name was Cutter, Mitch Cutter." When that prompted them to exchange another, even more alarmingly controlled look, she hastened to add, "I saw his identification; it was exactly like yours."

"I'm not sure what you saw or think you saw," the first man informed her calmly. "But Mitch Cutter does not work for the federal government."

"Then who does he work for?" asked Leigh in mounting distress.

"Anyone who needs his services," the other man replied. "Cutter is what's known as a bounty hunter, miss. A man who'll hunt anyone down for a price."

"That's ridiculous. I mean, who would pay to have me hunt——"

Her visitor cocked an eyebrow. "I think the answer to that is obvious, Ms. Bramwell. Don't you?"

It was obvious all right. And horrifying. Rudely slamming the window shut, Leigh braced herself against the door for support. It suddenly felt as if the bottom had been ripped out of her world and she was falling into a black, bottomless chasm.

Mitch had been lying to her, right from the start. He wasn't protecting her from DeMarco . . . he was working for him.

Chapter Seven

LEIGH STOPPED IN the middle of hurling things into the suitcase she'd unpacked only hours earlier and clasped her hands into a tense knot. What on earth was she doing?

Aside from the fact that she couldn't go on running away from this mess indefinitely, she had to bear in mind just whom she was preparing to run from. Fleeing from a hunter was probably the most foolhardy thing she could do. No matter how much she dreaded his return, she liked even less the thought of being Mitch Cutter's prey once again.

Beset by an avalanche of confusing, contradictory thoughts, she paced from her bedroom and down the wide staircase with its ornately carved banister. There was always the possibility that Mitch wasn't working for DeMarco, even though she couldn't think of another living soul who would hire a bounty hunter to track her down. But if he'd been sent after her to collect the money she owed or to warn her not to get chatty with the federal investigators, why hadn't he done either? Why had he instead gone to all the trouble of concocting a lie about his job? And why had he persisted in pretending he didn't know for sure that she had really borrowed the money?

Those were the questions Leigh allowed herself to formulate. Much more important to her were the ones she wasn't brave enough to ask herself, ones that had nothing to do with loans or investigations. But no matter how hard she tried, she couldn't will herself to forget that her relationship with Mitch had grown into something much more significant than that of two strangers forced to spend time together. Something she couldn't just coolly sweep aside, even if all the evidence did seem to say she had fallen in love with a lying mercenary who had ruthlessly hunted her down and stolen her heart for pay.

As her initial shock and panic began to fade, she gradually came to terms with the fact that sooner or later she was going to have to face the truth about Mitch, whatever it was. And the longer she waited for him to return, the more anxious she became—and the more determined to have answers to all her questions tonight. He would learn that she could be every bit as tenacious and relentless an inquisitor as he was. Her newly brave, aggressive mood was buoying . . . and it lasted until his Jeep roared into the driveway just before sunset.

When the doorbell chimed the first time, Leigh froze. Standing motionless in the living room, she quickly decided she'd rather get her answers later, tomorrow, anytime when she wasn't feeling so exhausted and ravaged from the emotional wringer this day had been. Frantically, she weighed the possibility that Mitch might just give up and go away if she didn't answer. But his rapid jabs on the bell, followed by a stretch of very impatient pounding, soon reminded her that he was not the sort to be easily dissuaded, and she began to inch her way toward the door.

"Leigh," he called out just as she neared the front hallway, "I know you're in there. Open the door. Now, Leigh."

"Now, Leigh," she mimicked, feeling a little flicker of defiance that was quickly extinguished by common sense. His voice held that clipped, implacable note she'd come to know and detest, and that meant this was not the best time to play taunt-the-hunter. It also meant it was probably useless to try to change his mind, but if the alternative was letting him in to do battle tonight, Leigh was stubbornly willing to try.

"Mitch?" she ventured, scrupulously avoiding the glimpse of him visible through the leaded glass window in the door. "I was . . . upstairs. Unpacking."

"Oh. Well, are you going to let me in or not?"

Exhaling deeply, she said in a breathy rush, "I'm not."

"I can't hear you, Leigh. Open the door."

"I said I'm not," she repeated, her voice brittle and just shy of a shout.

"Not what?"

"Not going to let you in."

"Why the hell not?"

"Because . . ." She hesitated, trying to gather the remnants of her courage. "Because it's late."

"Leigh, it's not even five o'clock in the afternoon."

"Well, it's been a long day."

"All right," he growled, "You've made your point."

"I have?"

"Right. It's been a long day because I got you out of bed early to drive back here without telling you beforehand what I had planned or asking your opinion of my idea. I can see now that you expected me to be more attentive this morning. And more . . . gallant or something. And I'm sorry."

"You're sorry?" she echoed, apprehension rapidly giving way to resentment. "You think I'm angry because you weren't attentive and gallant?" Try honest and trustworthy, she fumed silently.

"Right. And if you'll open the door, I'll show you how sorry I am."

"The same way you showed me last night that I was more than just an assignment to you?"

There was a long silence. Leigh was both sorely tempted and afraid to peek through the window at his expression.

"That's one way I could show you," he said finally, his quiet, controlled voice sending shivers dancing along her spine.

"No thanks," she drawled. "I'll take your word for it. And as for my not being merely an assignment, I'll take your word for that, too. After all, how could I be just an assignment to a man who doesn't even have a job? Or is hunting considered a full-fledged profession in your circles?"

This time the silence was shorter and infinitely more ominous.

"Open this damn door, Leigh," he ordered fiercely.

Her laughter was a harsh echo in the open hallway. "Sorry, Cutter, I'm through taking orders from you."

"That wasn't an order!" he bellowed. "It was a . . . hell, maybe it *was* an order. Now I don't know how you found out about me, but I do know you have a right to be angry. So scream at me, call me names, hit me with a rolling pin for godsake, but you are not going to lock me out here without giving me a chance to explain. I won't let you."

"You have no choice."

"The hell I don't!" he roared. "You're my woman!"

"One night in bed doesn't constitute a bill of sale," she retorted in fury. "And if you're staking your claim by right of capture, I'd say the spoils really belong to the man paying the bill. Just out of curiosity, how long did you plan to string me along before you handed me over to DeMarco?"

His snarled, violent expletive penetrated the solid wood door, and it was the only response Leigh got to her impulsive baiting. The next sound she heard came as no surprise. It was totally in character for Mitch to try and batter down whatever stood between him and what he wanted. But in this case it was also totally futile. One of the pleasant advantages of living in a solidly built castle, she mused smugly, was that you didn't even need a moat to keep intruders out—as Mitch was busy discovering the hard way.

His battering at the door produced only a muffled thud on the inside, followed by an anguished grunt. Leigh wanted to feel triumphant, to derive pleasure from his pain. Instead, she felt a quick stirring of some treacherous, protective instinct even stronger than anger.

"Mitch? Are you all right?" she cried, angling to look through the small window.

"No."

The distant sound of his voice was explained by the fact that he was slightly bent over, grasping his left shoulder with his other hand. But it was the look on his face, suddenly as white as the teeth clamped on his lower lip, that sent Leigh scrambling for the door latch.

Jerking it open, she rushed outside. "For heaven's

sake, don't you know better than to try to break down a heavy door—" She broke off abruptly, eyes narrowing suspiciously. "So help me, Mitch, if this was all a trick to get me out here..."

"It wasn't a trick," he assured her, straightening and rotating his shoulder cautiously. After a few seconds the color began to return to his face. His pained grimace was replaced by a crooked smile that did more to weaken Leigh's resolve than a thousand threats ever could have. "But I wish it had been. Then I wouldn't have hit the damn thing so hard and my shoulder wouldn't be throbbing as if I'd just got run over by a herd of cattle."

"You deserve every throb," she muttered.

He nodded solemnly. "Along with whatever else you decide to dish out as punishment. But could you at least hear my side of things first?"

Leigh hesitated. She was already out here anyway. And somehow he didn't look all that formidable, standing there kneading his sore shoulder with an expression that was every bit as grim as she felt.

"It won't do any good," she warned, "but I'll let you explain. I suppose you might as well come in."

"No." He shook his head firmly. "Why don't you get your jacket, and we can walk while I explain?" At the wary tightening of her stance, he added, "Believe me, it's safer that way than for me to be alone in the house with you right now. You were right when you said I'd try to prove things to you the same way I did last night. That's the way that comes easiest... the way I know best." His one-shouldered shrug was achingly vulnerable. "I think maybe it's time I tried to learn another way of dealing with a woman."

Leigh went back inside for her parka, and they walked in silence along the cobblestone path that circled around to the back. When they reached the steps leading down to the beach, Mitch placed a hand under her elbow.

"Careful," he cautioned, "these stones are slippery."

"Thank you." What was she thanking him for? She should be ranting at him. No, she shouldn't be out here strolling along a windswept beach with him at all.

"You're supposed to be explaining," she prodded stiffly as they turned in unison toward the natural cove a few hundred yards north of her place.

"I will. But first I want you to know that you're off the hook with DeMarco."

Leigh stopped dead in her tracks and whirled to face him. "What? How? I mean, I thought you were supposed to be—"

She broke off, caught between tides of relief and bewilderment . . . and doubt. She no longer knew what to think about anything, especially about Mitch Cutter's role in her troubles.

"I know what you thought. That I was working for DeMarco and that my promise to handle things for you was just a lie. Like the lie about my being a federal agent. I'm not," he acknowledged. "The closest I ever came were the years I spent as a detective with the state police, and I couldn't even hack that. I couldn't stand playing by all their stupid, official rules when the scum we were after were playing by a set all their own. And getting off scot-free most of the time."

He spoke quickly, flooding Leigh with way too many new thoughts for her to sort through. "I believed you," she said in a soft whimper. "Believed all of it." Lifting accusing blue eyes to his, she added, "You even had an I.D."

"Forged." One corner of his mouth quirked humorlessly. "It comes in handy in what I do now."

"You mean being a bounty hunter," she spat. "I know all about it."

"Not everything. For one thing, we're called recovery agents nowadays," he informed her.

"Oh, that makes all the difference in the world. I feel much better knowing you were paid to recover me instead of hunt me down like an animal."

Mitch scowled. "It wasn't like that. And I wasn't paid for it."

"Sure. You're the world's only volunteer bounty hunter."

"Recovery agent."

"Bounty hunter. And what a needy recipient you chose for your services," she drawled. "Eddie DeMarco, loan shark, gangster, and God knows what else."

"I was trying to say that I didn't *accept* payment for it. It's true that originally I was being paid to find you and—"

"How much?" she broke in.

Mitch met her gaze steadily, his eyes as opaque as the winter sea beyond. "Five thousand dollars."

Leigh shook her head in disbelief. "Why? I only owed him three. Even considering the twenty thousand he thinks I owed, I can't believe he'd spend five just to get his hands on me."

"It wasn't the money he was after, Leigh," explained Mitch. "He got a tip from some informant who works for the government that you knew more about him and his operation than you do, and he was just covering his bases. Evidently the Feds had the same idea, judging by how eager they were to have you on their side."

"But I don't know anything!" Leigh wailed. "Until Vinnie explained where the money came from, I didn't even know DeMarco existed."

"I know that, angel. And so does everyone else involved now. I spent the afternoon making sure of it. As of now both DeMarco and the government are much more interested in Vinnie as a star witness—a little case of returning the favor, since I'm sure he's the one who set you up in the first place to save his own hide. Your problems are over."

Leigh pressed her palms to her cheeks, almost afraid to believe it. "You mean DeMarco isn't looking for me anymore?"

He shook his head, a flash of white teeth appearing between dark mustache and beard. "Nope. And just for the record, I doubt he would have risked doing you any harm even if he'd found you. Just issued an uncomfortably forceful warning about letting his name slip in the wrong places."

"I thought that was why he'd sent you—to warn me."

"No. I never would have taken the job if that was the case. I had to fight my better judgment just to accept work from a sleazebag like DeMarco. I only did it because he said it was a personal matter, that you were his runaway mistress. And because it sounded like easy money," he added ruefully.

A wave of revulsion swept over Leigh. "What if I had been his . . . his mistress, and I was trying to get away from him? You would have dragged me back for a rotten five thousand dollars?"

His jaw hardened under her accusing glare. "Never. And I told him so upfront. He said he only wanted to know where you were and that he would go up and sweet-talk you back by himself. Then I saw you outside in the snow that first day, and I knew there was little chance you were involved with that creep. And there was no way I was going to let him know where you were unless it was what you wanted, too."

Leigh tried to juxtapose what he was telling her with what had happened the afternoon he rang her doorbell. It could be the truth. She turned and began walking slowly once more, aware that he was trailing along in silence, giving her time to digest everything he'd said.

"You could have just let it end there," she said, testing her thoughts out loud. "Gone back and told DeMarco you couldn't find me."

"I could have. But he would only have sent someone else—maybe someone who wouldn't find a snow angel as intriguing as I did. As I do." He settled his arm tentatively across her shoulders but surrendered with only a quiet sigh when she shrugged it away.

Bending down to pick up a piece of driftwood with his good arm, he continued quietly, "I came to your door hoping to find out a little more about you, about why a man like him was looking for you in the first place."

"And I did a good job of letting you know, didn't I?" groaned Leigh, remembering her panicked response to his appearance.

"Let's just say I had a good idea you weren't merely a piqued lover," he returned with a throaty chuckle. "And an even better idea that you couldn't possibly handle whatever was going on by yourself."

"Is that really why you stayed? To protect me?"

He halted and spun her around to face his exasperated expression. "I've been telling you that for days, woman. Is it finally sinking in?"

"You also told me a lot of other things," she reminded him pointedly.

"Out of necessity," he insisted. "I didn't even understand myself why I felt driven to take care of you, so how could I have explained it to you? And you never would have believed me anyway; you just would have thought I was some crazy jerk with ulterior motives."

"I thought that at times anyway," she revealed, not resisting this time when he caught her to him in a laughing, one-armed hug but not permitting herself to participate either.

"I'm not saying I didn't have a few *secondary* motives for wanting to stay with you," he drawled, his arm remaining stubbornly in place as they continued walking. "But concern for your safety was what drove me to lie about who I was. I knew you'd probably faint dead away if you found out I was actually a bounty hunter."

She giggled. "I almost did faint when those two real agents told me the truth about you."

Mitch shook his head with a disgusted sigh. "So that's how you found out."

"They came by this afternoon."

"They won't again," he asserted with quiet authority. "It's all behind you, Leigh. Even the three thousand you owe Demarco has been wiped out."

She gaped at him in amazement. "How did you manage that?"

Shrugging, he replied, "We sort of bartered about the fee he no longer has to pay me. It was mostly just lip service on his part. The amount of money is chicken feed to a guy like him compared to the security of knowing you're not plotting to testify against him. I'd venture he's as glad to be rid of you as you are of him."

Hands stuffed in her pockets, Leigh walked in silence. She knew she should probably protest the intimacy of his arm around her shoulders and his hard thigh brushing hers with each slow step, but she didn't have the energy. Or the desire, she acknowledged honestly.

A few feet in front of them lay a retaining fence, scrub

grass growing between slats that had been battered and broken by the summer's crowd of swimmers and the brutal forces of the winter. Soon now it would be replaced with a shiny new one, and the cycle of insidious abuse would begin again. She followed as Mitch guided her around it with the pressure of his body, trying not to think of the fact that this was probably the first and last time they would ever walk together like this. Would she ever forget the way his body felt against hers, she thought wistfully, so hard and lean and solidly, comfortingly masculine? Or the way he could warm and excite her with nothing more than the touch of his hot silver gaze? Probably not. The realization settled like an iceberg somewhere deep inside her.

His explanation for what he'd said and done struck Leigh as reasonable and true. She could forgive him for lying to her. She already had for the most part, especially when she considered his reasons. But she could never live with what he was. She had abhorred the danger inherent in his lifestyle when she'd still believed him to be a federal agent. This was far worse. This was dangerous and ungoverned and frighteningly solitary work.

But her resistance went far beyond the fear she would have to live with each day and night if they were to stay together. Something in her balked at the idea of a man's making his living in such a mercenary fashion. By preying on others, especially those who were already in trouble. True, most of those he dealt with probably deserved whatever happened to them. But the possibility that a few, like her, might have been unknowingly or unwillingly dragged into something dangerous, and that Mitch's involvement might add to their misery, was something she couldn't ignore.

If she tried to live with it, her hidden resentment would

leave their relationship as battle-weary and scarred as the fence lying broken behind them. And she could hardly expect her feelings to influence Mitch's choice of work. He was not, she knew well, a man used to making concessions or sacrifices for others. She moved beside him without speaking, her thoughts and welled-up tears a requiem for what might have been, until the silence grew thick and unbearable.

"Mitch," she began, then faltered, the victim of a suddenly dry tongue. He halted and turned to face her attentively. "First of all, I guess I should be thanking you . . . or something."

"Or something sounds just fine to me," he answered, smiling wickedly. "I wish I'd told you to grab a blanket when you went back for your jacket."

Refusing to respond to his tantalizing caress of a glance, she said, "I think that's something we have to talk about."

He tilted his head to one side and gazed at her absorbedly, his face only inches from hers, the wind ruffling the thick black waves of his hair. Leigh could hardly concentrate enough to string words together, let alone prepare one of the most excruciatingly difficult farewell speeches of her life.

"Would it help if I went first?" he asked gently.

Leigh nodded.

"I know I lied to you about who I was, and I'm sorry we had to start out that way, but if it came down to it, I'd do it all over again. As for the rest of it, everything that happened between us up there, it was all straight— no tricks, no ulterior motives—and I'm not sorry for any of it." Leigh studied the shoulder seam of his leather jacket while he scoured her face for some reaction. "I never meant to fall this hard. Hell, I still don't know what to make of it, but it happened, and that's that. Now, we can go on beating a dead horse for weeks about this lie I told, or you can forgive me."

She lifted her gaze to meet his. His eyes were soft, hopeful, not nearly as controlled as his voice. "I forgive you," she said softly. "And good-bye."

In the instant before she spun away, Leigh caught the look of relief that lit his darkly handsome face. But by the time he'd caught her arm and jerked her back to him, it had already been replaced by a more familiar expression of seething impatience.

"I forgive you and good-bye?" he stormed. "Is that your idea of a joke?"

"No. It's my idea of the quickest, kindest way to end this."

"Then you wasted your breath." His arms closed around her, bringing her fully against the unyielding contours of his body. There was something dark and irrepressibly sensual in his soft tone. "Because this isn't ending. In fact, it's hardly even begun. Open your mouth for me, angel."

Hands wedged uselessly between them, Leigh gasped, "Mitch, I—"

"Thank you," he breathed in the instant before his lips touched hers.

He feathered her mouth lightly at first, teasing, playing about the corners, as languorously as if she weren't struggling madly and straining as far away as his steel grip on her shoulders would permit. When the magic of his touch slowly began to dull her need to resist, he laughed softly deep in his chest and escalated his assault. His palms slipped around to cage her face, thumbs caressing her cheekbones even as they held her still for the passionate thrust of his tongue.

Leigh retreated, but the gesture was hollow, spiritless.

Her heart had already surrendered to his magic and was signaling frantically for her body to do likewise. Gradually, glorying in the slow, delicious process of defeat at his hands, she let herself be drawn into the erotic skirmish of warm, wet tongues. It was a skirmish in which Mitch was always in control. Sometimes fiercely, sometimes teasingly, but always he was the master, dictating the tempo and intensity, driving home the extent of his power and challenging her to resist.

Tilting his head, he brushed her cheek and temple with his lips, the scrape of his beard a different, roughly exciting sort of caress. Desire roared hotly through Leigh's veins.

"Do you still want to say good-bye to me?" he asked, angling back a bit to slant her a roguishly mocking grin.

Leigh shook her head. "No. But I should," she moaned.

"Should say good-bye?" he persisted, punctuating his words with exquisitely punishing nips of her bottom lip. "Or should want to?"

"Want to. I mean do it. Both." She let her flustered gaze slip away from his very satisfied masculine one. "I should say good-bye. This will never work. But when you touch me . . . make me feel this way . . . I can't. I don't want to."

"Good. Then that's settled: no more stupid good-byes. Now why don't you tell me why you think it won't work?"

"It just won't." She tugged her hands loose and clasped them behind his neck. It felt good, right to be touching him again. It was hard to concentrate on the reasons why it wasn't good and right. "I guess your work bothers me most."

He nodded, looking neither surprised nor very upset. "What bothers you about it?"

"The danger involved." When he grimaced impatiently, she added hurriedly, "But it's even more than that. Look, you came after me for no other reason than that there was five thousand dollars in it for you."

"That's not such a shabby reason by any standards."

"It's your standards that bother me. Granted it all worked out all right for me—"

"And me," he added huskily, dipping to touch the side of her throat with his tongue.

"But your next poor victim might not be so lucky."

His mouth twisted with wry humor. "I try to avoid thinking of them as victims."

"How do you think of the people you hunt?"

He shrugged uncomfortably.

"Prey?" she prodded. "Quarry? Game?"

"Subjects."

"Subjects?"

"Right, like subjects of investigations."

"Mitch, that's not a whole lot more compassionate than victims."

"I'm not in a compassionate business."

"Exactly. And I don't know if I can live with the business you're in."

He released a deep, tortured sigh and gazed over her head at the whitecaps dancing out beyond the breakers. The only sign that he even knew she was still there was his fingers moving on her shoulder muscles in a slow, steady caress.

"Would you believe me," he asked finally, swinging back to stare into her troubled eyes with gray ones that pleaded and cajoled, "if I told you I will not let my job be a problem between us?"

"It won't be your fault that it's a problem," explained Leigh. "Even if I could talk myself into thinking what you do isn't heartless and mercenary, there would always be the element of danger involved. I told you I hate taking risks. I think I'd also hate living with the fact that you take them . . . every day."

"You make it sound more exciting than it is," he told her with a dry inflection, "but it's nice to know you're concerned at least."

Something in his vulnerable expression, in the pleased smile that formed on his hard mouth at the thought that she cared enough to worry about him, brought the words from Leigh's heart to her lips.

"Of course I'm concerned. Don't you know that I love you?"

He looked thunderstruck, as if the possibility had never occurred to him, and for one endless, heart-shattering moment, Leigh thought he might be wishing it had never occurred to her either. Then he grinned, a slashing, wildly excited show of teeth that made her heart soar in response.

"I didn't let myself hope that you might eventually fall in love with me," he revealed to her silent astonishment. "I knew I could offer you protection. And I knew the sex was good, maybe good enough to forge a bond between us."

Leigh fought the laughter building inside. "You thought I would stay with you because you could protect me and the sex was good?"

His shrug held an endearing hint of sheepishness. "It would be more than a lot of couples have going for them. And besides, I don't know enough about love to think it might make a difference." Tipping her face up to his, he regarded her intently. "I've never said 'I love you' to a woman—any woman. Do you need to hear the words?"

Leigh's heart plummeted as what had seemed to be a

preamble to a declaration ended on a questioning note. "Not if you don't want to say them," she responded.

"It's not a matter of wanting to or not wanting to. If I felt them, I'd say them."

"So you don't feel them. At least now I know where I stand."

"No, you don't. How can you when I don't even know where I stand . . . or what I'm feeling?" His eyes softened another degree as he took in her disappointed look. "I do know that I feel something for you I've never felt before. If you want me to call it love, I will. To me, it's more important to know that there's a bond between us, a commitment. You're mine. And I want you with me forever."

A smile came to Leigh slowly. She supposed that was more of an impassioned declaration than some women ever got. And more than she would have thought Mitch capable of in those first stilted days of togetherness. This man, with his ill-at-ease way of expressing what he felt, meant more to her than any man with a string of glib endearments ever could. Of course, he did have this persistent tendency to refer to her like something he carried a deed for in his back pocket.

"If I'm yours," she ventured speculatively, "does that mean that I have the right to go around growling 'You're mine' about you, too?"

"Of course. I believe privileges should be fully reciprocal." He unleashed a blatantly suggestive smile. "All privileges. For instance, I was just about to bring you back to the house, tumble you onto the first bed I came to, and show you exactly what it means to belong to me." He leaned closer, communicating his desire for her through his eyes, his touch, his whole being. "But

I've just decided to give you the privilege of doing all that to me first."

Anticipation made Leigh's legs feel sluggish and awkward as they hurried back over the soft stretch of beach they'd just strolled along. It was a pleasure and a relief when they reached the staircase inside the house and Mitch swung her into his arms for the long climb.

"If all privileges are reciprocal," she teased, "how come I'm not carrying you?"

"I was wrong. Some rights I'll never relinquish, even temporarily. This one for instance," he added, bending his head to kiss her with leisurely enjoyment.

"You do realize, Cutter," she ventured, arching her neck in delight, "that at times you can be very possessive and domineering?"

Rounding the corner at the top of the stairs, he muttered against her throat. "You bring out the barbarian in me—do you care which room I choose?"

"Yes. Mine is the last one on the right, and sometimes I think barbarian is *all* there is in you."

He reached her room and paused in the doorway. The late afternoon sunlight that filtered through the crocheted curtains shadowed his face, but not so that Leigh couldn't read the intense longing in his gray eyes.

"Barbarian I may be," he vowed softly, "but I will never hurt you. And I will never let anything—anything!—stand in the way of what I've found with you. I've searched for so long without even knowing it; I'll never let you go."

Leigh accepted the veiled reference to his work with a silent nod. Maybe he was right about it, but even if he wasn't, she didn't want to think about it tonight. Tonight she wanted, needed, to know that they belonged to each other with the primal simplicity that seemed so important to Mitch as well.

With a long, fluid stride he crossed the room and lowered her to the center of the dark four-poster with its snowy chenille spread. While Leigh looked on unselfconsciously, her eyes bright with adoration and mounting desire, he methodically stripped off his clothes and lowered himself onto the bed beside her.

The sight of him heated Leigh's blood and made her breath rush out in short, shallow rasps. Her hands reached up to thread through his dark hair and feather over his strong shoulders and arms. She kept her touch light, wanting to stretch out the splendor, doling it out to herself in small snatches.

Mitch moaned softly when she dabbled a delicate pattern across his chest. "Ah, your hands feel so good on me. I need your touch to make me whole, Leigh."

She stroked the lean line of his hip, feeling powerful and womanly when he trembled in response.

"You make me ache, woman. I never knew what it was like to really ache with need until I met you, until I touched you and felt you shudder and melt in my arms."

Rolling to her side, Leigh burrowed her face against his shoulder, letting her teeth rake gently over his warm flesh. Her legs shifted restlessly as her hand swirled over the firm wall of his stomach.

"How do you feel when I touch you?" he whispered. At last he put his hand on her, his fingers sliding back and forth along the strip of skin exposed between her jeans and the shirt that had pulled free of her waistband.

"You make me feel good," she said in a hushed voice. His fingers were skating higher, over her ribs, sending rippling sensations all through her. "When you touch me you . . . oh, you don't know what you do."

"Tell me." It was a command, at once gentle and roughly exciting.

"You make everything inside go tense and watery at the same time." His smile made her braver, freer. "I feel as if I'm floating, and I never want it to stop."

He thrust his leg between hers, riding it high against the steady throbbing at the joining of her thighs. His palm brushed across her nipple, then made lazy circles around it until it was ripe and firm and Leigh was straining against him.

"Does that feel good?" At her breathy sound of agreement he captured the bud between his thumb and forefinger and rolled it firmly, watching her eyelids flutter and close in joyful response. "And this? I want to know exactly how you feel when I touch you, angel. I need to know that you need me every bit as much as I need you. *I* need the words."

"Oh, Mitch, I love you. And I need you. You must be able to tell how much."

"Show me. Tonight I want you to show me. Start by undressing for me, love. I want to watch you the way you watched me."

"I'll feel embarrassed with you watching me," Leigh protested, eyes downcast until Mitch lifted her chin.

"You shouldn't. You should feel beautiful and desirable and feminine. Because you are."

She lifted her hand from his chest and patted the curve of her hip. "You don't think I'm sort of, you know, chubby?"

Mitch fought the smile that threatened to slant his full mustache and regarded her with serious eyes. "Lord, no. You feel exactly the way a woman should feel—the way I want my woman to feel."

It was simple praise but heady, and more coolly than

she would have dreamed possible Leigh unbuttoned her pale blue shirt and pulled her arms out of it, baring her breasts to his appreciative gaze. A little less deftly, she worked open the jeans' snap and zipper, lifting her hips to skim them over her legs and kicking them away. When she reached for the lacy white panties that were all that shielded her from the heat swirling in Mitch's steadily darkening eyes, he reached out to stop her.

"Leave them . . . for now. I like the way you look with only your panties on."

Pressing her back flat on the mattress, he leaned over and began to touch her in the same fleeting, exploratory way she had touched him. Only he hadn't her patience, and his caresses soon grew bolder, sweeping from her breasts and tummy to her sensitive inner thighs. Leigh didn't mind. She was more than ready to have him love her fully, and she tried to signal her arousal by lifting into him with a kiss that was blatantly inviting.

Mitch responded with a low groan, opening his mouth to give her free access while his fingers coasted teasingly over the nylon-covered center of her desire. The mere hint of contact sent Leigh spinning higher on a wave of anticipation. Arching against his palm to coax it closer, she grazed his back with her nails. Immediately, Mitch reclaimed her mouth, this time with none of the passivity he'd displayed a few moments earlier. He used his tongue and teeth in devastatingly erotic plunges and bites, then scorched a path of rough kisses along her throat to her ear. The words he whispered there were low-pitched and rawly exciting, and Leigh twisted again, seeking relief from the pressure building in her lower body.

"Mitch, please, love me now," she gasped as his fingers continued the vague meanderings that were driving her crazy. "I need you."

"Show me how much, honey," he crooned close to her ear.

"I'm trying! What do you want me to do? Ravish you?"

He lifted his head, and in the rapidly darkening room his eyes gleamed with an enticing sensual challenge. "Yes, I think I'd like that. Ravish me, woman."

His tone was touched with humor, but the expression in his eyes was earnest, and Leigh realized in surprise that this was the reason for his teasing caresses tonight. He might not even know it himself, but tonight he did not want her to surrender. Tonight he was seeking the complete gift of love—the gift of herself freely given. It was as if by taking the initiative she would be accepting and sanctifying the bond between them.

Some feminine instinct that had long lain dormant rose boldly in Leigh, surpassing even that within which clamored for fulfillment. With everything in her that was woman, she reached out to please the man she'd accepted, chosen, as her own. The drive to give Mitch what he craved guided her hands and lips as they roamed over his body, seeking, revering, arousing.

Mitch fell back under her impassioned onslaught, reveling in her sometimes tender, sometimes fiercely demanding movements. His eyes closed, and the lines of his face tightened in an ecstatic blending of pleasure and pain as she let her body flow over his. Leigh felt his readiness and gloried in it, yet still she persisted, sliding her thigh along the inside of his, whispering without coyness the words that described the desire she felt for him.

Finally, with a savage exclamation of raw need, he lowered his hands to cup her buttocks. He ripped off her panties with an impatient groan and a deft motion she barely felt, and then he was lifting her over him, guiding her down until he was testing the power of his arousal at the damp softness waiting for him between her thighs. Leigh gasped out loud as, with the relentless urgency of a man whose patience has run out, he surged into her.

At first she watched in fascination the play of muscles across his chest and arms as he rose and fell beneath her in powerful thrusts. Then the passionate rhythm he set began to lure her, and she was moving against him and with him, each downward stroke igniting a new fire that licked through her, pushing her closer to the edge of the sensuous inferno she craved. Their movements blended perfectly, complementing each other. Mitch's every stroke was aggressive, marked by a fierce male hunger, and Leigh responded fully, with an urgency she had never known before.

Finally, just as the tension coiling within reached a point of unbearable intensity, Mitch worked his hand between their bodies and touched her intimately, in a way that sent her hurtling off into a world of pure sensation, like summer lightning crackling across a night-blackened sky. She was hardly aware of the turbulent release of his satisfaction that quickly followed. The only thing that pierced the rosy cloud that surrounded her was his voice, even deeper and rougher in passion, chanting her name as she collapsed on top of him.

When she finally summoned up the energy to move, Mitch followed, rolling to his side so he lay facing her. With one hand he idly brushed the long strands of dark hair that clung to her damp shoulders and chest. For a long time they lay without speaking, the silence too perfect to break.

Finally Leigh peered up at him with a drowsily mischievous gleam in his eyes. "Feeling ravished?"

"Quite. You never told me you were the aggressive, domineering type, too."

She executed a careless shrug. "Just one of my little secrets."

"I see. Well, I think it's time we discussed another one of your little secrets." When Leigh peered at him in bewilderment, he added, "I want to hear all about Joel."

Her bubble of laughter rose instinctively. "That's not a secret, Mitch. In fact, it's not even worth discussing."

"I think it is. I find everything about you fascinating." His fingers trailed along her throat to touch the still flushed tip of one breast. It responded instantly, and he smiled. "I think I'd be especially fascinated to hear about a man you once had as a lover—the *only* other lover you'll ever have."

A thrill shot through Leigh at the implication of his blunt remark. "I think you'll be more bored than fascinated. It was a long time ago, and not very titillating even then."

"Bore me," he ordered in a voice underlaid with steel.

Her lips twitched in amusement. Men could be awfully single-minded about some things, and she had a gut feeling that for Mitch, this was one of those things.

"I met Joel at a party about five years ago. We were both working in Newport and knew most of the same people. I guess that's one of the reasons we started seeing so much of each other: It felt natural, comfortable."

"How about sleeping with him?" Mitch interjected in a carefully offhand manner. "Did that feel natural, too?"

"It never felt anything like what I just felt with you, if that's what your ego wants to hear."

"It was," he acknowledged with a crooked grin. "My ego thanks you."

She smiled helplessly and rubbed her cheek against

his shoulder. "Anyway, Joel started talking about getting married, and it seemed like a good idea. We had so much in common and all."

"Did you marry him?" he asked, eyes opened a bit wider than usual.

"No. A few months before the date we'd set, Joel was offered a big job on the West Coast. And he took it."

"And?"

"And he never even bothered discussing it with me. He just assumed I'd trail along after him like some detached appendage."

Mitch winced, and Leigh knew he was thinking about that morning. "And because he was so callous as to not discuss his plans with you, you ditched him?"

"I ought to say yes to keep you on your toes," she laughed. "But no, it wasn't just that he hadn't considered my opinion. His accepting the job made me realize that I didn't love him enough to leave my family and friends and traipse across the country just to be with him. It was a blessing in a way."

"Did Joel think it was a blessing, too?"

"Not at first. I think his pride was hurt, and he would have liked having someone to share the adventure of settling in a new place, starting a new job. We parted friends though, and about a year ago he wrote to tell me he was getting married."

"Good. I don't relish the thought of having to battle lovers from your past. You're keeping me busy enough with your present adversaries."

Leigh attempted a haughty shrug. "You could have just let me handle this little matter myself. I would have thought of something." Arms folded across her chest she added, "Eventually."

"No doubt," countered Mitch dryly. "But you won't

ever have to worry about that again. From now on your battles are my battles, your problems my problems, your enemies my enemies."

"You make me sound like Calamity Jane," she groused. "Are you sure you don't want to rethink getting involved with me?"

"Positive. There's nothing in the world I'd rather do than take care of you." His hand, which had been lying still on her stomach, began to slide lower. "Well, maybe there's one thing I'd rather do . . ."

Leigh's hips rolled unconsciously. "Mmm? I wonder what that could be."

Leaning over to plant a quick, hard kiss on her mouth, he replied, "Feed you. I haven't eaten all day, and I'm starving. I'll bet you are, too."

"It wasn't exactly uppermost on my mind," she grumbled.

"Well, it should have been. You've been getting a lot of extra exercise lately," he pointed out with a wickedly suggestive flicker of a smile. "I don't want you getting *too* skinny."

She reached for her shirt. "All right, all right, you don't have to get carried away with ridiculous compliments. I'll go fix you something to eat."

"Absolutely not." He caught her hand as she was about to swing her legs over the side of the bed. "You've been cooking for me all week. It's time I spoiled you a little bit." Standing up to step into the black denims he'd tossed onto the foot of the bed, he asked, "Do you like Chinese food?"

She wrinkled her nose. "As long as it's not coconut chicken."

"No coconut, I promise." He finished tucking in his shirt and shrugging into his leather jacket and leaned over to kiss her again. "There's a Chinese restaurant with a great take-out menu about fifteen minutes from here. I'll be back before you have the table set."

After he'd left, Leigh got up and took a long, hot shower, emerging feeling relaxed and sated and at peace with the world. And with herself. The temperature had dropped in the house since the sun set, and she turned up the thermostat and dressed in a pair of soft gray corduroys and a warm pullover sweater. She decided they would eat in the kitchen, which always seemed cozier to her than the oversized dining room. Using her best china and wineglasses, she set the table, then trudged down to the cellar to select a favorite rosé from the supply of wine stored there in anticipation of the inn's opening. She had just placed a hurricane globe over a candle in the center of the table when the doorbell rang.

Her steps were eager and her heart was racing in anticipation as she hurried to answer it. It was insane, she scolded herself as she slipped open the lock; the man hadn't even been gone an hour, and she was as excited as if he were returning from a year at sea.

Yanking the door open, she greeted him with an irrepressible smile. "Mitch, that must have been the fastest fifteen-minute drive in history—"

The exclamation dwindled into a sharp gasp of dismay as her eyes locked with the taunting gaze of the man lounging against the doorframe.

"Sorry to disappoint you, baby," Vinnie Gilman drawled as he straightened and took a menacing step forward. "But it's just as well Cutter isn't here. After all, you and I have a lot to talk about."

Chapter Eight

DRIVEN BY SOME deep instinct for self-preservation, Leigh took a step backward. Then another. Too late, she realized she had just unwittingly given a very angry Vinnie carte blanche to enter her home.

He rapidly took advantage of her mistake. Stepping into the wide front hall, he swung the door shut behind him. As he ambled after her, Leigh unconsciously took stock of his disheveled appearance. His clothes were uncharacteristically rumpled, and his usually neat, dark hair was uncombed, as if he hadn't had time today. Even with her mind scrambling for some semblance of control, she couldn't help comparing him to Mitch. He was shorter, thinner. His face, she realized now, was too handsome and not nearly as strong or interesting or compelling as Mitch's. What had she ever found attractive about him? she asked herself in disgust.

Out loud she spoke firmly, trying to inject some calm

into her voice. "What do you want?"

Vinnie's laugh had a sharp, cruel overtone. "I already told you. We're going to talk. You seem to like talking— you sure did enough of it to your pal Cutter."

"I had no choice," Leigh countered, taking yet another backward step as he paced relentlessly onward. "I told you I didn't know how to handle—"

"I don't care *why* you talked," Vinnie interrupted loudly. "You did it. And I warned you about what happens to people who talk too much in this business."

Leigh swallowed hard. "But I'm not in your business. You of all people know I had no idea where that money came from."

"All I know," he said in a hostile, jeering voice, "is that you've made my life very uncomfortable. And I'm here to see if I can't do the same for you."

Leigh was finding it difficult to breathe, as if a giant steel band were encasing her chest. And she knew precisely what that band was made of: fear. Cold, stark fear. She had never thought of Vinnie as a dangerous man; if she had, she never would have dated him, even casually. But that's exactly how he looked now as he stalked her down the hallway and into the kitchen. Dangerous and desperate.

"Well, well," he crooned as they rounded the corner and his eyes fell on the carefully set table with its waiting candle and wine goblets. "Isn't this cozy? No wonder you were wearing such an ear-to-ear grin when you answered the door. I'm interrupting a romantic little interlude."

"That's right," Leigh agreed quickly. "Mitch will be right back."

"Too bad. Because we won't be here." He reached out and grasped her chin tightly with one hand, and at the same instant Leigh felt the kitchen counter against her back. She was trapped. "You and I are going to take a little ride."

Panic, raw and paralyzing, washed through her. At least as long as she was here, there was the possibility that Mitch or someone else might arrive to rescue her. Alone with Vinnie in a car, she would be completely at his mercy.

"I had been hoping that we'd have a little time alone together first, though," he was saying, sliding his finger and thumb to opposite sides of her jaw hinge and pressing. "You know, for old times' sake. How long till Cutter will be back?"

Leigh thought quickly. "I'm not sure. He had to drive to the city for something. He said he'd be back by ten or so."

Vinnie followed her gaze to the clock on the wall near the stove. "That gives us a couple of hours—if you're telling the truth. And you'd better be. Because if your new boyfriend surprises us, I just may have to hurt him." He pinched her jaw tighter until she winced. "Sure you don't want to change your mind about when he's coming back?"

Leigh shook her head as emphatically as his hold permitted. Mitch was her only hope. And she had a strong hunch that if he tangled with Vinnie, he would not be the one to get hurt.

"Good. I'd hate to miss out again on what you were so damn stingy with all the time we were dating." His other hand forced its way into her hair, yanking her head back so she was staring straight into his eyes. They were cold. And hungry, Leigh realized frantically. "Now I don't want to hear you say, 'No, Vinnie,' or 'I'm tired, Vinnie,' or 'Not tonight Vinnie,'" he instructed coldly.

"I just want you to stand there and make me think you're enjoying every minute of this—or else."

Her lips parted unwillingly as he drilled his fingers into her jaw, and then his mouth was on hers, grinding harshly, his tongue snaking out and filling her mouth with the taste of beer and stale cigarettes. It was obscene. Even more so because her senses were still alive with the taste and feel of Mitch.

Uncaring of what his "or else" might mean, Leigh shoved at his chest as hard as she could. She'd rather face his abuse than succumb like a coward to this degradation. In desperation she lifted her foot, kicking wildly at his shins.

"You bitch!" he snarled, jerking on her hair so hard that tears flooded her eyes. "I said act like you're enjoying it."

"No. I hate it, and I hate you." Her voice was unnaturally high, saturated with the fear rushing through her. "I won't let you do this to me."

"And even if she would, I wouldn't."

Vinnie froze. Slowly, Leigh twisted her head against his painful hold and gazed over his shoulder. Mitch was standing in the hallway entrance to the kitchen, his stance loose limbed and relaxed, one arm hoisting the brown paper bag of food. His poise was a facade, Leigh realized immediately, sensing the lethal threat behind his nonchalance and in his voice that sounded more inflexible and harsh than she had ever heard it.

He didn't make a move toward where Vinnie held her imprisoned against the counter, his hand still painfully twisting her hair. But his presence alone was enough to short-circuit the terror that had been pounding inside her like something wild and uncontrollable. She didn't know how Mitch was going to handle this, but she knew he would. Her confidence didn't waver even as Vinnie slowly released her hair, only to spin her in front of him as a shield while he wrenched a gun from beneath his jacket.

"Still feeling brave, Cutter?" he taunted, waving the gun close to Leigh's face.

From across the room, Mitch watched him press the barrel of the small black revolver against her cheek, and he swore he could feel its cold, deadly touch as if it were happening to him. He forced aside the distractingly vivid sensation and concentrated on making mental notes about the other man's size and position and the distance between them.

"Because if you are," Vinnie continued, "we could both lose out—permanently. After all, I had every intention of returning the lady to her rightful owner . . . when I was through with her, of course."

His chuckle and the snide twist he put on the word *lady* grated on Mitch's already raw nerves, causing him to spend a tremendous amount of effort to keep from hurling the bag in his arms straight at the other man's head. He couldn't. He couldn't do any of the potentially dangerous things he would do if he were here alone, if Leigh weren't standing with her back pressed to that creep, her eyes pleading with him to do something.

He refused to look at her eyes again. His sense of control was already alarmingly shaky. Seeing the glistening proof of just how terrified she was would only feed his frustration and could end up putting her in more danger. And that was the last thing he wanted to do.

In the space of a heartbeat, when he'd walked in and found her being mauled by Gilman, the last stones in his wall of resistance had tumbled around him. He hadn't even known he was resisting. Hadn't realized that the wary, untrusting habits he'd learned from a lifetime of

loneliness were all that was keeping him from acknowl-
edging his true feelings for Leigh. The sight of her struggling against that animal had sent the truth storming
through him in a desperate, crushing wave and taught
him all he needed to know about love. He loved her,
more than he loved the idea of drawing another breath
or waking up tomorrow morning. Without her he didn't
even want to wake up.

For both their sakes, he had to play this one safe.

"Okay, Cutter," Vinnie was saying, "now that you
know how serious I am, why don't you walk over to the
table—real slow like—and put that bag down. And don't
try anything stupid."

"Why should I?" Mitch asked, starting toward the
table with short, unhurried steps.

"I thought maybe you planned to make a habit of
coming to this lady's rescue."

"I'm not getting paid to play hero."

"No? Well, nobody paid you to screw up my life
either, but you did it," sneered Vinnie.

Mitch lowered the bag to the table and turned with a
shrug. "That was to my advantage at the time." He flicked
an intentionally suggestive glance in Leigh's direction,
fighting a wave of revulsion when her captor responded
with a lewd grin. "Now it appears my advantage lies
elsewhere."

"You're a real cagey bastard, aren't you?" Vinnie said.
"It seems to me you're the only one coming out of this
thing ahead. You collect a nice fee from DeMarco for
chasing her down; then you do a number on me to get
her all nice and thankful and into your bed." He tightened
the arm clamped just below Leigh's breasts, drawing her
up on her toes to listen to his snarling accusations. "And
all those months you held me off, like you were some

damn saint. Then this guy shows up to bail you out, and in a few days you're giving it all away. It just goes to show, doesn't it, Cutter, that every woman's a whore if the price is right."

Mitch regarded him coldly. "I guess you should know, Gilman. You've probably had a lot more dealings with whores than I have."

Vinnie stared back at him through narrowed eyes, obviously trying to figure out if he'd just been insulted or paid a real man's compliment. "Yeah, well, this is one whore I plan to deal with in my own way." He jerked Leigh closer. "Only I don't like an audience, so I guess we'll just have to stop somewhere along the way, honey."

"Are you two going somewhere?" Mitch asked in a laconic, almost disinterested tone.

"Yeah, we're going somewhere. It seems I don't have a car at my disposal this evening. I had to leave mine parked outside my mother's when I slipped out the back way. Seems a couple of DeMarco's boys were waiting out front to talk with me. Of course that doesn't come as a surprise to you, does it, Cutter?"

"No. I'm only surprised to learn you have a mother."

"Shut up!" he snapped. "Your mouth has already gotten me in enough trouble. First you whispered in DeMarco's ear and got him breathing down my neck, and then the Feds come around clamoring for me to tell them everything I know."

Shrugging, Mitch countered, "That's your problem now. If you don't want to talk, don't talk."

"They're not giving me much choice. Either I talk, or they're going to make it look on the street like I talked. Either way I'm finished around here."

"That's a shame. We'll miss you."

"Speak for yourself," Vinnie drawled with chilling

satisfaction. "Leigh here is going to be seeing a lot more of me . . . real soon now."

Mitch lounged back against the kitchen table and folded his arms across his chest. "Just one thing about this bothers me, Gilman," he announced. "I figured you for the type who didn't let people walk all over him."

"Yeah. So?"

"So if you're so convinced I'm the one responsible for your troubles, why are you taking it out on Leigh? And letting me just walk away?"

"I'm not taking it out on anyone," he bit out. "And I'm certainly not stupid enough to risk being slapped with a felony charge just for the satisfaction of breaking a few of your bones. I came here because I need a ride to a friend's place in Boston, and as a driver Leigh offers, uh, fringe benefits that you don't."

"If you're expecting Leigh to drive you, I'm afraid you're in for a big disappointment."

Vinnie had begun dragging Leigh in the direction of the back door. Now he stopped and uttered a very belligerent, "Why's that?"

"Because the battery in her car is dead. I tried jumping it myself earlier."

"Then we'll take your car."

Mitch shook his head. "She can't drive it; it's a stick."

Vinnie muttered a quick, vivid expletive. "Then we'll switch the damn batteries."

"Wrong size," Mitch countered calmly.

"Damn!"

Mitch hazarded a glance at Leigh and saw her wet her lips nervously. Not now, angel, he groaned silently. You've kept silent all this time; be a good girl just a while longer until I can get us out of this.

"I have an idea," she said in a quavering voice that

pierced Mitch's resolve to remain unemotional.

"I'm sure Gilman has an idea of his own,". Mitch responded quickly.

Vinnie waved the gun in his direction. "Shut up and let her talk. What's your bright idea?"

Mitch could feel her eyes on him as the silence in the room grew thick. She was questioning, waiting for a signal of some sort that he couldn't give. He was afraid it would only alarm Gilman or confuse her further.

"Well? Let's hear it!" exploded Vinnie, giving her ribs a cruel squeeze.

"I . . . I was going to say that you could take Mitch's Jeep and drive yourself to Boston. Then you'd have a car there in case you decided to go somewhere else or come back here or something."

"But then I wouldn't have any fun on the way, would I, honey?" Eyes riveted on Mitch, he ducked his head and nuzzled the side of her neck. "No, Cutter was right: I do have a better idea. We're all going to go in the Jeep. Cutter can keep his eyes on the road while he drives, and you and I will have plenty of privacy in the back seat."

A feeling of exhilaration shot through Mitch. This was exactly what he wanted, to get Gilman moving so he could take advantage of any slipup, any distance he might put between Leigh and that gun. Only he couldn't let Gilman know how badly he wanted to go along.

Maintaining his lounging position against the table, he said harshly, "Hold on, Gilman. What's in it for me if I drive you where you want to go?"

Vinnie swung the gun around so it was pointed directly at Mitch's forehead. "You get to go on living long enough to enjoy this little morsel again," he drawled, nudging Leigh's breasts with his arm.

"I think I'll go on living one way or the other. You said it yourself, Gilman: You don't want to risk a felony charge just for a ride to Boston."

"What I want to do and what you might force me to do are two different things." Keeping the gun trained on Mitch, he started inching toward the door again. "I need to get to my friend's place tonight. And you're going to get me there. Now move. Open the door and start walking—real slow—to your car."

Mitch did as Vinnie ordered, wishing he could give Leigh a reassuring glance as he passed in front of them, but it was too risky. He would just have to hope she trusted him enough to know that everything he was saying and doing was necessary to keep Gilman from guessing just how precious the woman he was holding hostage was to him. God, when this was over, he was never, ever, going to leave her alone again.

The narrow walkway outside the back door was almost indiscernible in the dark. The street lights were too far away to cast any illumination here, and Gilman had harshly overridden Leigh's offer to turn on the floodlights. Mitch had wanted to throttle her when she suggested it. The darkness had a neutralizing effect on the gun their captor was wielding—a minuscule effect, granted, but it was all they had going for them at the moment.

That and the fact that the path they were treading was even more treacherously slippery now than it had been in the warmer afternoon. Mitch remembered that as they walked in a single file toward where his car was parked, and he breathed a fervent prayer that Leigh would remember as well. Especially as they reached the point where the path dropped in a gradual slope to the front drive. She was walking directly behind him, with Gilman bringing up the rear, and Mitch wondered if he should turn and issue a warning about the walk after all. If Leigh should lose her footing now, it could startle Gilman enough to make him fire.

He turned to speak to them over his shoulder at the same time that Leigh gave a short yelp of surprise. He sensed more than saw her going down behind him, and he whirled around without thinking to break her fall. But she was already arching backward, and in the instant that was all the time he had before his instincts took over, Mitch realized she was only faking the fall to throw the man behind her off guard.

"What the—"

Gilman's annoyed growl was cut short as Leigh twisted and fell against his chest with both arms outstretched. The impact was enough to send his feet flying out from under him on the slick walk, and for a second both of them lay sprawled at Mitch's feet in the darkness. With a swift, explosive motion Mitch lunged, kicking the gun out of Gilman's loosened grasp, then hauling him to his feet to savor the longed for, satisfying contact between his fist and the other man's jaw.

For the first time since he'd arrived at the house, he forgot all about Leigh and gave full rein to the violent impulses he had been struggling to contain. He pummeled Gilman's face and chest, his fury only intensifying with each scattered blow he received in turn. When his foe's foot slipped from under him, forcing him to one knee, Mitch followed him down and continued the fight on the stretch of muddy lawn between the walk and drive.

The fight quickly turned vicious once they hit the dirt and Vinnie realized he couldn't win fairly. Mitch was confident his opponent couldn't win period, but it satisfied some basic urge in him to continue battering the man who'd terrorized his woman, to hear the solid sound of his balled hand slamming against flesh. He probably would have continued until Gilman passed out or begged for mercy if Leigh hadn't called a halt to things in a voice that was suddenly very clear and composed.

"Stop it!" she commanded from somewhere on the driveway below them. "Both of you stop it."

Panting, his lungs aching from the effort of drawing in air, Mitch gave Gilman one final shove face first into the soft earth and struggled to his knees.

"You, too, Vinnie!" called Leigh. "Get up."

He obeyed, with difficulty. Grunting and pressing a hand to his blood-splattered nose, he lumbered to his feet. Mitch was already standing, dabbing at the trickle of blood coming from a split bottom lip when he noticed that Leigh was holding Vinnie's gun and had it pointed in the general direction of the two men.

"I'll take that now, Leigh." He began to stretch out his hand, only to have Vinnie's wild laugh cut him short.

"Not if she's smart, you won't," he said. "She knows exactly what you are now, Cutter: a cold-hearted bastard who's only interested in saving his own skin." Swinging his gaze to Leigh, he went on contemptuously, "He didn't do a damn thing to try and save you, baby, not even when he knew what I had planned for you. Truth is, he probably would have enjoyed looking on."

With a savage oath Mitch swung around, ready to shut Gilman's mouth for the rest of the night, until Leigh's voice rang out sharply in the darkness.

"Stop! Mitch, move away from him."

Seething with anger and frustration, he turned to glare at her. "Leigh, this has gone on long enough."

"I couldn't agree more," she countered solemnly.

"Good. Then hand me the gun like a good girl."

"Don't do it, baby," interjected Vinnie. "How do you

know he's not still working for DeMarco? You could be jumping out of the frying pan and into the fire."

Mitch watched, horrified and enraged as she appeared to weigh carefully what Vinnie had suggested. "Leigh, dammit, that's crazy, and you know it."

"How do you know it, Leigh?" taunted Vinnie.

"Shut up!" Mitch snarled at him over his shoulder, but the question burned him like acid.

How did she know he was telling the truth? Just because he said so? A man who'd lied to her once that she knew of and who'd told her a bunch of other things that she actually had no concrete reason for believing? A man who'd accepted her sweet declaration of love and then said he didn't know if he loved her in return? A man who never said the right thing or even knew what kind of things a woman liked to hear?

Even back there in the house he'd probably made a mess of things. Maybe she'd expected him to do something flashy and brave, to act like some knight in shining armor for Pete's sake. She probably didn't realize that a stunt like that—like the one she'd pulled—could have gotten her killed. So he had forced himself to play it safe, and now she was holding a gun on him and wondering if he had told her the truth about any of it.

Well, she wasn't going to get away with it. She was his woman, and if she loved him as she claimed to, she would believe him even if he didn't do such a great job of making himself understood.

"Leigh," he said with all the quiet authority he could muster, "I want you to hand me that gun right this minute."

"I . . . I really don't think I should, Mitch," she replied, still clenching it Hollywood style, in both fists, in a way that made him very uneasy. "It might be dangerous."

"Woman, it's going to be a lot more dangerous for you when I get my hands on you if you don't hand it over right now!"

"You're shouting, Mitch. That means you're about to lose your temper, and I don't think that's the best state of mind for someone holding a gun to be in."

"Wrong!" he bellowed. "It means I've already lost my temper. Now give me the gun!"

"I can't. I'm afraid."

That blunt admission shattered what was left of Mitch's quiet control. "You have no reason to be afraid of me, dammit. I love you, for godsake."

"You do? Really?"

"Yes, really. Now give me the damn gun."

From behind him Gilman issued a thoroughly disgusted sigh as her shadowy form moved closer in the darkness.

"Of course, Mitch," she said in a voice that was sweet and compliant. "There's no need to shout."

It was nearly midnight by the time they got around to reheating the Chinese food Mitch had bought. The friend from the state police whom Mitch had notified had arrived, along with the federal investigators working on the case, and spirited Vinnie away with quiet efficiency.

"I'm glad there weren't a lot of flashing lights and sirens," Leigh told him as they munched on eggrolls and sweet-and-sour shrimp up in her bedroom. Somehow the kitchen wasn't her favorite spot to relax in just then. "It would have been bad publicity for the inn."

"It would have been worse publicity for the inn," Mitch informed her dryly, "if that gun had accidentally gone off with you holding it and killed somebody."

"Like you?"

"That thought did cross my mind."

Leigh shuddered and put down her fork. "Oh, Mitch, I would have died right along with you. I was so concerned that you might shoot Vinnie if you got your hands on the gun that I didn't stop to think of all the other things that could possibly go wrong."

His mouth quirked in wry amusement. "I still can't believe you thought I had so little control over my temper that I would kill the man in cold blood."

"If you could have seen the fury seething from you down there in the kitchen, you would have thought the same thing."

"And the whole time I thought I was being the epitome of cool detachment."

"Darling, cool, detached men do not grind their teeth."

He scowled at a piece of shrimp for a full ten seconds before clamping his teeth on it. "I'm glad Gilman didn't see me grinding my teeth," he declared a moment later. "It would have ruined my whole plan."

"You mean *my* whole plan," corrected Leigh. "Remember, I was the one who wrestled the gun away from him."

"Angel, I don't think knocking the man down strictly qualifies as wrestling the gun away from him. If you want to get technical, I actually kicked it away from him."

"Who ended up with it?"

Mitch sighed. "You."

"I rest my case."

"Good. Because I'm sick of talking about Vinnie Gilman and guns and all the rest of it."

"Even wrestling?" She reached out and toyed with the buttons of his shirt.

"I'll never get tired of wrestling as long as you're the one I get to pin."

"Kind of sure of yourself, aren't you?" Leigh asked, feeling excitement stir inside.

Mitch lifted the tray that lay between them and put it on the nightstand. "There's one way to find out."

"I'm not sure I like the idea of being pinned," she protested with mock concern.

"I guarantee you'll like it better than being beaten, which was my first inclination when you stood out in that driveway defying me."

Leigh fluttered her long lashes demurely. "It is unfortunate that I seem to have developed this irksome defiant streak just when I've found a man who demands unquestioning obedience."

She fought hard to suppress a smile as he peered at her with dark eyebrows lowered ominously. "You're laughing at me. You think it's funny that I expect my woman to trust me and accept my judgment in matters I happen to know more about."

"I do trust you. I gave you the gun, didn't I?"

"Only after you pulled that crazy stunt of tackling Gilman."

"You're referring, of course, to the crazy stunt that may have saved our lives?"

"Okay. It happened to work—but it was a risk you never should have taken."

Leigh rose to her knees to loop her arms around his neck. "That's something I learned tonight, Mitch. Sometimes taking a risk isn't a matter of choice. I was so afraid that if we got into that car, in the mood you were in, you'd do something foolish."

His mouth slanted in amusement. "So you decided to

do something foolish first?"

"It didn't seem foolish at the time," she countered with a piqued expression. "It seemed an extremely practical way to avoid potential disaster."

Mitch tugged her closer, letting his lips slide lazily over hers. "And I'm thankful you did it." The expression in his eyes grew stern for a second. "Furious but thankful. And proud. I know how you feel about taking a risk, any risk, and that was one colossal way to break in."

"Believe me, I don't plan to make a habit of it," she assured him, shifting so she lay in the crook of his arm, her head cushioned by his chest. "In fact, now that I've seen a little of the dangerous aspect of your work first-hand, I think I hate it even more."

"I think I'm starting to agree with you a little bit." He pulled her back down as she started to twist in his arms. "And don't look at me that way."

"What way?"

"Kind of hopeful . . . and starry-eyed. I'm thirty-five years old, Leigh, and I'm not qualified to do much besides what I do."

"I think you could do anything you chose to do."

He chuckled. "I think love must be blind, but thanks for the vote of confidence. What I can do is start to concentrate on the kind of cases I've shied away from in the past."

"What kind of cases?" asked Leigh.

"Safe, boring ones. Like tracking runaways. They can pay very well, too, which is something I never cared about very consistently before."

Leigh placed her palm on his chest, loving the sure, steady feel of his heart pounding against her fingertips and hating the idea of condemning him to a lifetime of safe, boring cases against his will.

"Mitch, I don't want you to do something you hate just for me."

"It's not for you," he replied instantly. "It's for both of us. I thought I'd go crazy tonight when I watched him holding that gun to your head. I realized later that that's what you'd be going through every time I left the house if I keep on the way I am." His hand slipped from her shoulder to nestle in the warm shelter of her neck. "When you love somebody as much as I do you, you want to spare them that kind of pain. And you want to be around to go on loving them, too. The risks just wouldn't be worth taking anymore, angel."

Leigh pressed her cheek tightly against him; sweeping over her was a relief and happiness so pure she almost couldn't bear it. "Mitch, you really meant it when you said you loved me?"

"Of course I meant it. What did you think?"

Her shoulders lifted in a small, sheepish shrug. "That you wanted me to hand over the gun and—"

Before she could finish, he'd rolled a hundred and eighty degrees, landing on top of her with an expression of barely leashed menace. "If you thought that, you don't know me at all," he growled.

Leigh put every ounce of her love into the smile she gave him. "Mmm. But just think of all the fun we can have getting acquainted."

His expression hardened, then softened, and finally a smile worked its way awkwardly across his mouth. Leigh's own smile deepened as she remembered just how new all this teasing and playfulness was for Mitch.

"You have a point," he conceded gruffly. "And I think we should get started right away." He lowered his head to nibble the side of her throat.

"Why?" Leigh murmured, shivering in response to the sensual rasp of his beard against her skin. "Is there a time limit?"

"Uh-huh. One lifetime—that's all I have to offer you."

"I accept."

"I want it all, Leigh," he told her, his voice as steely as the gray eyes flaming darkly above her. "The church and the license and my ring on your finger—"

"And mine on yours," she interjected. "Remember your theory of reciprocity."

"I think I may spend the rest of my life regretting I ever said that," he groaned, but his expression was dreamily content as his hands slid down to cup her full breasts.

Leigh felt her nipples tighten in response, and at the same time the rest of her body began to feel warm and receptive. Tracing the strong contours of his back with loving hands, she whispered, "I'll spend the rest of my life making sure that you don't."

His hard thigh slipped between hers, pressing firmly against her, turning her desire into a hot liquid rush and her thoughts into chaos.

"I love you, Leigh." The words were spoken with reverence and passion and pure masculine possession. "I know I'm not the man of your dreams—hell, I know I'm not even close—but I'll do my best to make you happy."

Leigh reached up and threaded her hands through the thick black waves of his hair. "I think my dreams may have been decidedly lacking."

He shook his head stubbornly even as his fingers began inching her sweater higher, over the curve of her breasts. "No. I know a woman wants a man who's romantic and gallant..."

"And passionate and exciting and sexy," she added.

His eyes narrowed speculatively. "You mean that stuff matters to women, too?"

"Cutter, you have a lot to learn about women."

"Teach me." He moved his hips in a slow, provocative circle over hers, the feel of him alluringly hard against her softness.

"The first thing you should know is that a woman loves to feel wanted." Reaching for the top button on his shirt, she worked it open, then moved on to the others. "As much as I may tease you about it, all that fiercely possessive stuff is very arousing to a woman on some basic, unspoken level."

"It is?" He drew a ragged breath as she finished unbuttoning his shirt and tugged it loose from his pants, slipping her fingers inside the snug waistband to stroke his belly in the process.

"Mmm. Definitely. She might not like to admit it, even to herself, but there's something wildly exciting about having the man you love stake his claim on you..." She slid the shirt off his shoulders with a long, silky caress. "Having him remind you that you belong to him and only him..." Laughing softly, she rose enough to bring her breasts into warm, delicious contact with his bare chest. "Being made a willing captive to the passion you create together."

Shifting beneath him, Leigh settled her leg between his and arched it at the knee, pressing against him with exquisite force, bringing him as much pleasure as he brought her. Mitch shuddered and closed his eyes briefly. When he opened them again, Leigh saw a hot silver reflection of the love and happiness and desire that surrounded her like velvet chains.

"I think that all sounds...ah, fantastic," he murmured, his thickened voice like sandpaper against her skin. "But I can't help wondering, are you my captive? Or am I yours?"

"Who cares?" Leigh whispered, smiling as she surrendered to the velvet chains and to the man who forged them so masterfully that he was now bound as surely as she was . . . for a lifetime.

Second Chance at Love ®

___ 0-425-07977-5	**BRIEF ENCOUNTER #252** Aimée Duvall	$2.25
___ 0-425-07978-3	**FOREVER EDEN #253** Christa Merlin	$2.25
___ 0-425-07979-1	**STARDUST MELODY #254** Mary Haskell	$2.25
___ 0-425-07980-5	**HEAVEN TO KISS #255** Charlotte Hines	$2.25
___ 0-425-08014-5	**AIN'T MISBEHAVING #256** Jeanne Grant	$2.25
___ 0-425-08015-3	**PROMISE ME RAINBOWS #257** Joan Lancaster	$2.25
___ 0-425-08016-1	**RITES OF PASSION #258** Jacqueline Topaz	$2.25
___ 0-425-08017-X	**ONE IN A MILLION #259** Lee Williams	$2.25
___ 0-425-08018-8	**HEART OF GOLD #260** Liz Grady	$2.25
___ 0-425-08019-6	**AT LONG LAST LOVE #261** Carole Buck	$2.25
___ 0-425-08150-8	**EYE OF THE BEHOLDER #262** Kay Robbins	$2.25
___ 0-425-08151-6	**GENTLEMAN AT HEART #263** Elissa Curry	$2.25
___ 0-425-08152-4	**BY LOVE POSSESSED #264** Linda Barlow	$2.25
___ 0-425-08153-2	**WILDFIRE #265** Kelly Adams	$2.25
___ 0-425-08154-0	**PASSION'S DANCE #266** Lauren Fox	$2.25
___ 0-425-08155-9	**VENETIAN SUNRISE #267** Kate Nevins	$2.25
___ 0-425-08199-0	**THE STEELE TRAP #268** Betsy Osborne	$2.25
___ 0-425-08200-8	**LOVE PLAY #269** Carole Buck	$2.25
___ 0-425-08201-6	**CAN'T SAY NO #270** Jeanne Grant	$2.25
___ 0-425-08202-4	**A LITTLE NIGHT MUSIC #271** Lee Williams	$2.25
___ 0-425-08203-2	**A BIT OF DARING #272** Mary Haskell	$2.25
___ 0-425-08204-0	**THIEF OF HEARTS #273** Jan Mathews	$2.25
___ 0-425-08284-9	**MASTER TOUCH #274** Jasmine Craig	$2.25
___ 0-425-08285-7	**NIGHT OF A THOUSAND STARS #275** Petra Diamond	$2.25
___ 0-425-08286-5	**UNDERCOVER KISSES #276** Laine Allen	$2.25
___ 0-425-08287-3	**MAN TROUBLE #277** Elizabeth Henry	$2.25
___ 0-425-08288-1	**SUDDENLY THAT SUMMER #278** Jennifer Rose	$2.25
___ 0-425-08289-X	**SWEET ENCHANTMENT #279** Diana Mars	$2.25
___ 0-425-08461-2	**SUCH ROUGH SPLENDOR #280** Cinda Richards	$2.25
___ 0-425-08462-0	**WINDFLAME #281** Sarah Crewe	$2.25
___ 0-425-08463-9	**STORM AND STARLIGHT #282** Lauren Fox	$2.25
___ 0-425-08464-7	**HEART OF THE HUNTER #283** Liz Grady	$2.25
___ 0-425-08465-5	**LUCKY'S WOMAN #284** Delaney Devers	$2.25
___ 0-425-08466-3	**PORTRAIT OF A LADY #285** Elizabeth N. Kary	$2.25

Prices may be slightly higher in Canada.

Available at your local bookstore or return this form to:

SECOND CHANCE AT LOVE
Book Mailing Service
P.O. Box 690, Rockville Centre, NY 11571

Please send me the titles checked above. I enclose _____ Include 75¢ for postage and handling if one book is ordered; 25¢ per book for two or more not to exceed $1.75. California, Illinois, New York and Tennessee residents please add sales tax.

NAME _____

ADDRESS _____

CITY _____ STATE/ZIP _____

(allow six weeks for delivery)   SK-41b

COMING NEXT MONTH
IN THE
SECOND CHANCE AT LOVE SERIES

ANYTHING GOES #286 by Diana Morgan
Zany inventor Kyle Bennett challenges Angie Carpenter's
title as Supermom by waging a housekeeping
competition with his robot...then sweeping Angie off her feet!

SOPHISTICATED LADY #287 by Elissa Curry
Despite her highfalutin name and prim good looks,
Abigail Vanderbine has trouble controlling her
all-too-natural impulses around wholesomely sexy
peanut-butter manufacturer Mick Piper!

THE PHOENIX HEART #288 by Betsy Osborne
Nothing's quite proper in Alyssa Courtney's proper life once
laid-back cartoonist Rade Stone showers her with gifts
and advice...then transforms her into a shameless wanton!

FALLEN ANGEL #289 by Carole Buck
Rock star Mallory Victor, floundering in a glitzy, ephemeral
world, yearns to trade the limelight for a love life with
rock-solid David Hitchcock, the man she's sure can save her.

THE SWEETHEART TRUST #290 by Hilary Cole
Collaborating with writer Nick Trent becomes infinitely
complicated when Kate Fairchild inherits
a crumbling Victorian mansion...and seizes the chance to
domesticate Nick into the man of her dreams.

DEAR HEART #291 by Lee Williams
Charly Lynn thinks no *real* man is as sensitive as
Robert Heart, her favorite lovelorn columnist.
Certainly not Bret Roberts, with his devilish chimpanzee
and presumptuous come-ons!

QUESTIONNAIRE

1. How do you rate _____
   (please print TITLE)
   ☐ excellent   ☐ good
   ☐ very good   ☐ fair   ☐ poor

2. How likely are you to purchase another book
   in this series?
   ☐ definitely would purchase
   ☐ probably would purchase
   ☐ probably would not purchase
   ☐ definitely would not purchase

3. How likely are you to purchase another book by
   this author?
   ☐ definitely would purchase
   ☐ probably would purchase
   ☐ probably would not purchase
   ☐ definitely would not purchase

4. How does this book compare to books in other
   contemporary romance lines?
   ☐ much better
   ☐ better
   ☐ about the same
   ☐ not as good
   ☐ definitely not as good

5. Why did you buy this book? (Check as many as apply)
   ☐ I have read other
      SECOND CHANCE AT LOVE romances
   ☐ friend's recommendation
   ☐ bookseller's recommendation
   ☐ art on the front cover
   ☐ description of the plot on the back cover
   ☐ book review I read
   ☐ other _____
      _____
      _____

(Continued...)

6. Please list your three favorite contemporary romance lines.

_____
_____
_____

7. Please list your favorite authors of contemporary romance lines.

_____
_____
_____
_____
_____
_____
_____

8. How many SECOND CHANCE AT LOVE romances have you read? _____

9. How many series romances like SECOND CHANCE AT LOVE do you <u>read</u> each month? _____

10. How many series romances like SECOND CHANCE AT LOVE do you <u>buy</u> each month? _____

11. Mind telling your age?
    ☐ under 18
    ☐ 18 to 30
    ☐ 31 to 45
    ☐ over 45

☐ Please check if you'd like to receive our <u>free</u> SECOND CHANCE AT LOVE Newsletter.

We hope you'll share your other ideas about romances with us on an additional sheet and attach it securely to this questionnaire.

• •

Fill in your name and address below:
Name _____
Street Address _____
City _____ State _____ Zip _____

Please return this questionnaire to:
SECOND CHANCE AT LOVE
The Berkley Publishing Group
200 Madison Avenue, New York, New York 10016